KING OF DIAMONDS

A DARK MAFIA ROMANCE

RENEE ROSE

BURNING DESIRES

Published in the United States of America

Renee Rose Romance

Editor: Maggie Ryan

ACKNOWLEDGMENTS

Thank you so much for reading my mafia romance. If you enjoy it, I would so appreciate your review—they make a huge difference for indie authors.

My enormous gratitude to Aubrey Cara and Lee Savino for their beta reads and for Maggie Ryan's rush job on editing. I love you guys!

Thanks also to the amazing members of my Facebook group, Renee's Romper Room. The kink talk and support inspire me every day!

CHAPTER 1

$\mathcal{S}$ondra

I TUG down the hem of my one-piece, zippered house-keeping uniform dress. The Pepto Bismol pink number comes to my upper thighs and fits like a glove, hugging my curves, showing off my cleavage. Clearly, the owners of the Bellissimo Hotel and Casino want their maids to look as hot as their cocktail girls.

I went with it. I'm wearing a pair of platform-heeled wrap-arounds comfortable enough to clean rooms in, but sexy enough to show off the muscles in my legs, and I pulled my shoulder-length blonde hair into two fluffy pigtails.

When in Vegas, right?

My feminist friends from grad school would have a fit with this.

I push the not-so-little housekeeping cart down the

hallway of the grand hotel portion of the casino. I spent all morning cleaning people's messes. And let me tell you, the messes in Vegas are big. Drug paraphernalia. Semen. Condoms. Blood. And this is an expensive, high-class place. I've only worked here two weeks and I've already seen all that and more.

I work fast. Some of the maids recommend taking your time so you don't get overloaded, but I still hope to impress someone at the Bellissimo into giving me a better job. Hence dressing like the casino version of the French maid fantasy.

Dolling myself up was probably prompted by what my cousin Corey dubs, *The Voice of Wrong.* I have the opposite of a sixth sense or voice of reason, especially when it comes to the male half of the population.

Why else would I be broke and on the rebound from the two-timing party boy I left in Reno? I'm a smart woman. I have a master's degree. I had a decent adjunct faculty position and a bright future.

But when I realized all my suspicions about Tanner cheating on me were true, I packed the Subaru I shared with him and left for Vegas to stay with Corey, who promised to get me a job dealing cards with her here.

But there aren't any dealer jobs available at the moment—only housekeeping. So now I'm at the bottom of the totem pole, broke, single, and without a set of wheels because my car got totaled in a hit and run the day I arrived.

Not that I plan to stay here long-term. I'm just testing the waters in Vegas. If I like it, I'll apply for adjunct college teaching jobs. I've even considered substitute teaching high school once I have the wheels to get around.

If I'm able to land a dealer job, though, I'll take it because the money would be three times what I'd make in the public school system. Which is a tragedy to be discussed on another day.

I head back into the main supply area which doubles as my boss' office and load up my cart in the housekeeping cave, stacking towels and soap boxes in neat rows.

"Oh for God's sake." Marissa, my supervisor, shoves her phone in the pocket of her housekeeping dress. A hot forty-two-year-old, she fills hers out in all the right places, making it look like a dress she chose to wear, rather than a uniform. "I have four people out sick today. Now I have to go do the bosses' suites myself," she groans.

I perk up. I know—that's *The Voice of Wrong*. I have a morbid fascination with everything mafioso. Like, I've watched every episode of *The Sopranos* and have memorized the script from *The Godfather*.

"You mean the Tacones' rooms? I'll do them." It's stupid, but I want a glimpse of them. What do real mafia men look like? Al Pacino? James Gandolfini? Or are they just ordinary guys? Maybe I've already passed them while pushing my cart around.

"I wish, but you can't. It's a special security clearance thing. And believe me—you don't want to. They are super paranoid and picky as hell. You can't look at the wrong thing without getting ripped a new one. They definitely wouldn't want to see anyone new up there. I'd probably lose my job over it, as a matter of fact."

I should be daunted, but this news only adds to the mystique I created in my mind around these men. "Well, I'm willing and available, if you want me to. I already finished my hallway. Or I could go with you and help? Make it go faster?"

I see my suggestion worming through her objections. Interest flits over her face, followed by more consternation.

I adopt a hopeful-helpful expression.

"Well, maybe that would be all right...I'd be supervising you, after all."

Yes! I'm dying of curiosity to see the mafia bosses up close. Foolish, I know, but I can't help it. I want to text Corey to tell her the news, but there isn't time. Corey knows all about my fascination, since I already pumped her for information.

Marissa loads a few other things on my cart and we head off together for the special bank of elevators—the only ones that go all the way to the top of the building and require a keycard to access.

"So, these guys are really touchy. Most times they're not in their rooms, and then all you have to worry about is staying away from their office desks," Marissa explains once we left the last public floor and it was just the two of us in the elevator. "Don't open any drawers—don't do anything that appears nosy. I'm serious—these guys are scary."

The doors swish open and I push the cart out, following her around the bend to the first door. The sound of loud, male voices comes from the room.

Marissa winces. *"Always knock,"* she whispers before lifting her knuckles to rap on the door.

They clearly don't hear her, because the loud talking continues.

She knocks again and the talking stops.

"Yeah?" a deep masculine voice calls out.

"Housekeeping."

We wait as silence greets her call. After a moment the door swings open to reveal a middle-aged guy with slightly graying hair. "Yeah, we were just leaving." He pulls on what must be a thousand dollar suit jacket. A slight gut thickens his middle, but otherwise he's extremely good-looking. Behind him stand three other men, all dressed in equally nice suits, none wearing their jackets.

They ignore us as they push past, resuming their conversation in the hallway. "So I tell him…" The door closes behind them.

"Whew," Marissa breathes. "It's way easier if they're not here." She glances up at the corners of the rooms. "Of course there are cameras everywhere, so it's not like we aren't being watched." She points to a tiny red light shining from a little device mounted at the juncture of the wall and ceiling. I've already noticed them all over the casino. "But it's less nerve-wracking if we're not tiptoeing around them."

She jerks her head down the hall. "You take the bathroom and bedrooms, I'll do the kitchen, office and living area."

"Got it." I grab the supplies I need off the cart and head in the direction she indicated.

The bedroom's well-appointed in a nondescript way. I

pull the sheets and bedspread up to make the bed. The sheets were probably 3,000 thread count, if there is such a thing. That may be an exaggeration but, really, they are amazing.

Just for kicks, I rub one against my cheek.

It's so smooth and soft. I can't imagine what it would be like to lie in that bed. I wonder which of the guys slept in here. I make the bed with hospital corners, the way Marissa trained me to, dust and vacuum, then move on to the second bedroom and then the bathroom. When I finish, I find Marissa vacuuming in the living room.

She switches it off and winds up the cord. "All done? Me too. Let's go to the next one."

I push out the cart and she taps on the door of the suite down the hall. No answer.

She keys us in. "It is way faster having you help," she says gratefully.

I flash her a smile. "I think it's more fun to work as a team, too."

She smiles back. "Yeah, somehow I don't think they would go for it as a regular thing, but it's nice for a change."

"Same routine?"

"Unless you want to switch? This one only has one bedroom."

"Nah," I say, "I like bed/bath." Of course that's because of my all-consuming curiosity. There are more personal effects in a bedroom and a bathroom, not that I saw anything of interest in the last place. I didn't go poking around, of course. The cameras in every corner have me nervous.

This place is the same as the last, as if they'd paid a decorator to furnish them and they were all identical. High luxury, but not much personality. Well, from what I understand, the Tacone family—at least the ones who run the Bellissimo—are all single men. What can I expect?

I make the bed and move on to dusting.

From the living room, I hear Marissa's voice.

"What?" I call out, but then I realize she's talking on the phone.

She comes in a moment later, breathless. "I have to go." Her face has gone pale. "My kid's been taken to the ER for a concussion."

"Oh shit. Go—I've got this. Do you want to give me the keycard for the last suite?" There are three suites on this top floor.

She looks around distractedly. "No, I'd better not. Could you just finish this place up and head back downstairs? I'll call Samuel to let him know what happened." Samuel's our boss, the head of housekeeping. "Don't forget to stay away from the desk in the office."

"Sure thing. Get out of here." I make a shooing motion. "Go be with your kid."

"Okay." She digs her purse out from the cart and slings it over her shoulder. "I'll see you tomorrow."

"I hope he's all right," I say to her back as she leaves.

She flings a weak smile over her shoulder. "Thanks. Bye."

I grab the vacuum and head back into the bedroom. When I finish, I hear male voices in the living room.

"Hope you can get some sleep, Nico. How long's it been?" one of the voices asked.

"Forty-eight hours. Fucking insomnia."

"G'luck, see you later." A door clicks shut.

My heart immediately beats a little faster with excitement or nerves. Yes—I'm a fool. Later, I would realize my mistake in not marching right out and introducing myself, but Marissa has me nervous about the Tacones and I freeze up. The cart stands out in the living room, though. I decide to go into the bathroom and clean everything I can without getting fresh supplies. Finally, I give up, square my shoulders and head out.

I arrive in the living room and pull out three folded towels, four hand towels and four washcloths. Out of my peripheral vision, I watch the broad shoulders and back of another finely dressed man.

He glances over then does a double-take. His dark eyes rake over me, lingering on my legs and traveling up to my breasts, then face. *"Who the fuck are you?"*

I should've expected that response, but it startles me anyway. He sounds scary. Seriously scary, and he walks toward me like he means business. He's beautiful, with dark wavy hair, a stubbled square jaw and thick-lashed eyes that bore a hole right through me.

"Huh? Who. The fuck. Are you?"

I panic. Instead of answering him, I turn and walk swiftly to the bathroom, as if putting fresh towels in his bathroom will fix everything.

He stalks after me and follows me in. "What are you doing in here?" He knocks the towels out of my hands.

Stunned, I stare down at them scattered on the floor. "I'm...housekeeping," I offer lamely. Damn my idiotic fascination with the mafia. This is not the freaking

8

Sopranos. This is a real-life, dangerous man wearing a gun in a holster under his armpit. I know, because I see it when he reaches for me.

He grips my upper arms. "Bullshit. No one who looks like"—his eyes travel up and down the length of my body again—"*you*—works in housekeeping."

I blink, not sure what that means. I'm pretty, I know that, but there's nothing special about me. I'm your girl-next-door blue-eyed blonde type, on the short and curvy side. Not like my cousin Corey, who is tall, slender, red-haired and drop-dead gorgeous, with the confidence to match.

There's something lewd in the way he looks at me that makes it sound like I'm standing there in nipple tassels and a G-string instead of my short, fitted maid's dress. I play dumb. "I'm new. I've only been here a couple weeks."

He sports dark circles under his eyes, and I remember what he told the other man. He suffers from insomnia. Hasn't slept in forty-eight hours.

"Are you bugging the place?" he demands.

"Wha—" I can't even answer. I just stare like an idiot.

He starts frisking me for a weapon. "Is this a con? What do they think—I'm going to fuck you? Who sent you?"

I attempt to answer, but his warm hands sliding all over me make me forget what I was going to say. *Why is he talking about fucking me?*

He stands up and gives me a tiny shake. "Who. Sent. You?" His dark eyes mesmerize. He smells of the casino—of whiskey and cash, and beneath it, his own simmering essence.

"No one...I mean, Marissa!" I exclaim her name like a secret password, but it only seems to irritate him further.

He reaches out and runs his fingers swiftly along the collar of my housekeeping dress, as if checking for some hidden wiretap. I'm pretty sure the guy's half out of his mind, maybe delirious with sleep deprivation. Maybe just nuts. I freeze, not wanting to set him off.

To my shock, he yanks down the zipper on the front of my dress, all the way to my waist.

If I were my cousin Corey, daughter of a mean FBI agent, I'd knee him in the balls, gun or not. But I was raised not to make waves. To be a nice girl and do what authority tells me to do.

So, like a freaking idiot, I just stand there. A tiny mewl leaves my lips, but I don't dare move, don't protest. He yanks the form-fitting dress to my waist and jerks it down over my hips.

I wrest my arms free from the fabric to wrap them around myself.

Nico Tacone shoves me aside to get the dress out from under my feet. He picks it up and runs his hands all over it, still searching for the mythical wiretap while I shiver in my bra and panties.

I fold my arms across my breasts. "Look, I'm not wearing a wire or bugging the place," I breathe. "I was helping Marissa and then she got a call—"

"Save it," he barks. "You're too fucking perfect. What's the con? What the fuck are you doing in here?"

I'm confounded. Should I keep arguing the truth when it only pisses him off? I swallow. None of the words in my head seem like the right ones to say.

He reaches for my bra.

I bat at his hands, heart pumping like I just did two back-to-back spin classes. He ignores my feeble resistance. The bra is a front hook and he obviously excels at removing women's lingerie because it's off faster than the dress. My breasts spring out with a bounce, and he glares at them, as if I bared them just to tempt him. He examines the bra, then tosses it on the floor and stares at me. His eyes dip once more to my breasts and his expression grows even more furious. "Real tits," he mutters as if that's a punishable offense.

I try to step back but I bump into the toilet. "I'm not hiding anything. I'm just a maid. I got hired two weeks ago. You can call Samuel."

He steps closer. Tragically, the hardened menace on his handsome face only increases his attractiveness to me. I really am wired wrong. My body thrills at the nearness of him, pussy dampening. Or maybe it's the fact that he just stripped me practically naked while he stands there fully clothed. I think this is a fetish to some people. Apparently, I'm one of them. If I wasn't so scared, it would be uber hot.

He palms my backside, warm fingers sliding over the satiny fabric of my panties, but he's not groping me, he's still working efficiently, checking for bugs. He slides a thumb under the gusset, running the fabric through his fingers. My belly flutters.

Oh God. The back of his thumb brushes my dewy slit. I cringe in embarrassment. His head jerks up and he stares at me in surprise, nostrils flaring.

Then his brows slammed down as if it pisses him off I'm turned on, as if it's a trick.

That's when things really go to shit.

He pulls out his gun and points it at my head—actually pushes the cold hard muzzle against my brow. *"What. The fuck. Are you doing here?"*

I pee myself.

Literally.

God help me.

I freeze and pee trickles down my inner thighs before I can stop it. My face burns with humiliation.

Now, the anger and indignation I should've had from the start rushes out. It's the exact wrong moment to get lippy, but I glare at him. "What's *wrong* with you?"

He stares at the dribble on the floor. I think he's going to... Well, I don't know what I think he'll do—pistol whip me or sneer or something—but his expression relaxes and he shoves the gun in its holster. Apparently, I finally gave the right reaction.

He grips my arm and drags me toward the shower. My brain is doing flip flops trying to get back online. To figure out what in the hell is happening and how I can get myself out of this very crazy, very fucked up situation.

Tacone reaches in and turns on the water, holding his hand under the spray as if to check its temperature.

My brain hasn't turned back on, but I wrestle with his grip on my arm.

He releases it and holds his palm face out. "Okay," he says. "Get in." He draws his hand out of the shower and jerks his head toward the spray. "Clean up."

Is he coming in there with me? Or is this really just about washing off?

Fuck it. I *am* a mess. I kick off my shoes and step in, panties and all.

I don't know how long I stand there, drowning in shock. After a while, I blink and awareness seeps back in. Then I freak out. What in the hell is happening? What will he do with me? Did I really just pee on his floor? I want to die of embarrassment.

Keep it together, Sondra.

Jesus Christ. The mafia boss who stands on the other side of the shower curtain thinks I'm a narc. Or a spy or rat—whatever they call it. And he just stripped me down to my panties and pointed a gun at my head. Things could only get worse from here. A sob rises up in my throat.

Don't cry. Not a good time to cry.

I stumble back against the tile wall, my legs too rubbery to stand. Hot tears spill down my cheeks and I sniff.

The shower curtain peeps open right by my face and I jerk back. I didn't know he was standing right outside it.

~

Nico

MINCHIA. Shit.

My remaining doubts about the girl evaporate when I hear her crying. If I made a mistake, it's a really fucking big one. Because I seriously don't want to have to explain to my head of HR why I stripped one of our employees and held a gun to her head. *In my bathroom.*

I've seriously gone off the deep end this time. The insomnia is fucking with me—making me paranoid and itchy. I need to get my little brother Stefano out here to help me run the place so I can sleep at least an hour a night. He's the only one I trust.

"Hey." I make my voice softer. The girl's standing under the spray of water, soaking her Harley Quinn pigtails and the pair of light blue satin panties she's still wearing.

Fuck if I don't want to yank them right off her and see what's underneath.

I'm pretty sure she's in shock, and who could blame her? I terrify my employees on my best days and that's without tearing off their clothes and flashing a weapon.

Her chest shudders as she lets out a silent sob and it gets under my skin, same way her sniffle did. Somehow, I don't think undercover feds or any kind of professional would pee on my floor and cry in my shower. So yeah. I seriously fucked up here.

I reach past her and shut off the water, soaking the entire arm of my suit jacket in the process. "Hey, don't cry."

A better man might apologize, but until I'm one hundred percent sure there's not something off here, I keep it in. I yank the shower curtain open, and pull her out to stand on the bath mat while I wrap one of the towels from the floor around her. Because she seems to still be in shock, I hook my thumbs in the waistband of her wet panties and tug them down her trembling legs. I must not be as depraved as I think, because I somehow manage not to look at what she keeps under them when I lower to a squat and grip her ankle to help her step out of the dripping fabric.

I toss them in the garbage can. Earlier, I threw a towel over the place where she peed, and her eyes dart there now.

I know she's gotta be completely humiliated by it, but the truth is, she's not the first person I've made piss themselves. I guess she's the first female. The only one I'm sorry for scaring.

She's trying to stifle her sobs, which, of course, only turns them into snorts and choked gasps. Now I really feel like a first-class asshole.

"Aw, *bambina*." I grab the two corners of the towel, and pull her against me. Her wet skin dampens my suit, but all I can think about is how soft her lush, naked form is against my body. The exhaustion in my limbs ebbs, cleared by the flames of white-hot desire. "Shh. You're okay."

She trembles against me, but her sobs quiet.

"Did I hurt you?"

She shakes her head, her wet pigtails splattering a drop of water onto my cheek. Her gaze tracks to it. A loose section in the front flops over her eyes.

I shift my grip on the towel to one hand and use the other to brush the hair back from her face. "You're okay," I repeat.

She blinks up at me with long-lashed blue eyes. I love having her up close and captive where I can study her better. She's as beautiful as I originally thought, with porcelain skin and high cheekbones. It's not just beauty that makes her special. There's some other quality that makes her seem so out of place here. A fresh-faced innocence. Yet she's not overly naive or young. She's not dumb, either. I can't put my finger on it.

I don't release her. I don't want to. The heat of her body radiates through my damp clothes and crowds my mind with the dirtiest of thoughts. If I were a gentleman, I'd leave the room and let her get dressed, but I'm not. I'm an asshole with a hotel casino to run.

And I still don't know who the hell this girl is or how she ended up in my suite. And seriously, heads are going to roll for this. Even more because the girl suffered for it.

Right. If my brain were working better, I might acknowledge I'm the only one who can take blame for that part, especially since I'm still holding her naked and captive.

"It's just a girl who looks like you doesn't normally clean rooms in Vegas," I offer as the lamest excuse ever. It's true, though. I'm sure there are more girls like her out there. But I don't see them around here. All I see are the fake-boobed hustlers trying to work some angle. The professionals. Women who use their bodies like weapons. And I have no problem with them. I'm happy to use their bodies, too.

But this one—she's different.

Her full berry lips part, but she doesn't say anything.

I can't keep my hands to myself. I run my thumb across her lower lip, trace it back and forth over the plump flesh.

Her pupils dilate, giving me encouragement to keep touching.

"A girl like you is usually on the stage—some kind of stage—even if it's just a gentleman's club."

Her eyes narrow but I don't shut up.

"Girl like you could make a shit ton selling herself." Mary, Queen of Peace, I want to kiss the girl. I lower my lips but manage to stop above hers. A kiss would definitely not be welcome. I may be a scary prick, but I don't force myself on women. "You know how much a guy like me would pay for a night with you?"

This time I really went too far. She tries to yank back from me. I don't release her, but I do lift my head. She presses her lips together a moment before saying, "May I go?"

I ease back, but shake my head. "No." It's a decisive syllable, short and curt.

She flinches. The dilated pupils narrow back to fear. I don't like her afraid nearly as well as I like her trembling and soft, open to me, the way she was a moment ago. It's a subtle distinction, though, because I do love the power position of having her here, at my mercy.

"I still need some answers." I back her toward the sink counter, then pick her up by the waist and plop her bare ass down on the cool marble top. The towel flaps open when I release her, and I get another eyeful of her perfect, full breasts as she scrambles to find the corners and pull it closed.

I shake my head to clear the fresh flood of lust rocketing through me. My cock's gone rock hard. I'm a man used to getting everything he wants, which usually includes women. The fact that this one isn't available makes me want her even more. "Seriously," I mutter. "I'd pay five large for a night with a girl like you." Even as I say it, I know I'd never want her that way. I'd want to coax the willingness out of this one.

And that's my strangest thought yet. Because I never, ever spend time dating.

"I'm not a prostitute," she snaps, blue eyes flashing.

Her anger pulls me out of my sleep-deprived fantasy. I blink several times. "I know. Just saying you could make a lot of money in this town."

I shake my head. What the fuck am I saying? I don't want this girl to become one of those women.

And she just wants to get the hell out of here. So I need to get back to my interrogation.

"Who are you and why are you here?"

She draws in a shaky breath. "My name is Sondra Simonson. My cousin, Corey Simonson, works here as a dealer. She got me this job in housekeeping while I wait for something better to open up." She speaks rapidly, but it doesn't sound rehearsed. And it has enough details to ring true. "Marissa is my boss, and I offered to help her clean the rooms up here because the regulars are out sick. Her kid got a concussion and she had to leave me up here by myself. All I did was clean." She lifts her chin, even though her pulse flutters at a frantic pace in her neck.

I wait for her to go on, not because I'm still that suspicious, but because I like hearing her talk.

She babbles on, "I just moved here from Reno...I taught art history at Truckee Meadow Community College."

I tilt my head, trying to assimilate this new information. It only adds to the wrongness of this girl being in my room. "Why is an art history professor working as a goddamn maid in my hotel?"

"Because I have terrible taste in men," she blurts.

"That right?" I have to work to keep from smiling. I lean my hip up against the counter between her spread thighs. When she blushes, I know she must be thinking about how close her pretty little bare pussy is to the part of me most eager to touch her.

I'm even more fascinated by this lovely creature now. What kind of guy does an art history professor fall for?

She swallows and nods. "Yeah."

"You follow a guy here?"

"No." She lets out her breath with a sigh. "I bailed on one. Turns out we had an unshared interest in polyamory."

I lift an eyebrow. She's studying me right back, her blue eyes intelligent now that the fear is wearing off.

"Let's just say finding him banging three girls in our bed will be forever burned into my mind. So"—she shrugs — "I took our car and headed to Vegas. But karma got me because it got totaled when I arrived."

"How is that your karma?"

"Because half that car belonged to Tanner and I stole it."

I shrug. "Whose name was on the title?"

"Mine."

"Then it's your car," I say, like I'm the guy who makes the final ruling on all things to do with her ex. "So that still doesn't explain why you're in my bathroom."

Or maybe it did. My brain is still short-circuiting from lack of sleep. The real truth is probably that I don't want to let her go. I'd like to string her up in my room and interrogate her with my leather flogger all night long. I wonder how that pale skin would look with my hand prints on it.

Too much, Tacone. I try to pull back. The room swims and dips as my vision trails. Fuck, I need sleep.

She blinks rapidly. "Because you won't let me leave?"

I was right. She's smart.

The corners of my mouth twitch.

"Housekeeping is the only place I could get a job on short notice. I'd rather work as a dealer. Think you can hook me up?" Now she's getting sassy.

Funny, I don't have the urge to take her down a peg the way I usually do with employees. Unless, of course, it involves her naked and at my mercy.

Oh yeah. I already set that up.

But the suggestion of her working as a dealer irritates the fuck out of me. I don't know if it's because she'd be ruined by Las Vegas in a month, or because I really want to keep her in my room. Cleaning my floors. Naked.

"No."

She flinches because I say the word too hard. I'm definitely having a difficult time modulating my behavior. But she just shrugs. "Well, this is temporary, anyway. Just until I earn enough to get a new car and find a teaching job."

Okay, even not trusting my instincts, I think she's who she says she is. Which means I have no good reason to keep her prisoner here. I step back and take another long perusal of her now that I know more about her. Seriously. I want to keep her.

But considering the things I just did to her, she'll probably quit the second she leaves my suite. I point to her crumpled dress and bra on the floor. "Get dressed."

Before I do or say anything else to traumatize the girl, I leave the bathroom, shutting the door behind myself.

 *ondra*

WELL. That was interesting. My knees wobble when I stand. What will he do now? Am I free to go? I pull on my clothes with shaking hands and zip my dress all the way up, even though he's already seen my breasts.

The wet panties are in the trash bin, so I go commando.

I decide the best course of action is to hold my head high and march right out of there. Because there's no way in hell I'm sticking around to finish cleaning his suite after what just went down. I grab the doorknob and take a breath. Here goes nothing.

He stands in the hallway in front of my cart, talking on his cell phone. Blocking my exit.

Damn.

I catch my breath again at how scary-sexy he looks—

the delicious way he fills the expensive suit, his thick, dark hair that curled up at the edges, the penetrating dark eyes.

He ends the call and drops his phone in his suit pocket. "Your story checked out, at least for now. I'll be digging further." His dark eyes glitter but the menace I sensed there before has vanished.

I straighten my back, which draws his gaze down to my tits. "You won't find anything."

The corners of his mouth curve faintly. He watches me like a lion watches prey. Hungry. Sure of himself. He shakes his head, almost ruefully. "Girl who looks like you...shouldn't be cleaning rooms," he mutters.

I march past him, giving him a wide berth. "Yeah, you said that earlier."

The guy just totally *violated* me. Stripped me naked and watched me pee on his floor. I need to get the hell out of here and never come back. Forget working for the mafia. I have a life worth living...somewhere else. Somewhere far from Vegas.

I push the cart, even though I never finished cleaning his bathroom. *Just get the hell out, Sondra.*

"Hold up," he barks. "Leave the cart. Tony will take you home."

A tap sounds at the door and a huge guy with a wire in his ear walks in. Judging by the bulge at his sides, he packs as much heat as Tacone.

Fuckity fuck fuck.

I step back, shaking my head. *Oh hell, no.* I'm not getting in a car with this guy so he can shoot me in the head and drop me off a pier. Okay, there are no piers in Las Vegas. The Hoover Dam, then. I'm not that stupid.

"Relax." Tacone must've seen the blood drain from my face. "You'll get home safely. You have my word. Hold up just a minute." He walks out of the living room and into his office.

I grab my purse from the housekeeping cart. "I-I'll just take a bus," I call out after him and head toward the door, hoping to skirt past Tony. "That's what I usually do."

Tony doesn't budge from his position in front of the door.

"*You're not taking the fucking bus.*" Tacone sounds so scary I stop in my tracks. He returns holding an envelope, which he hands to Tony and murmurs something I didn't hear. "Go with Tony." It's a command, not an option. Tony's stood there stony-faced the whole time. Now, he lifts his chin at me.

I walk to the door, trembling like a leaf. Tony opens it, ushers me through and shuts it again. I dart a glance up at the beefy man beside me. Tony drops a huge paw on my nape. "You're okay."

Seriously? Does this guy care about my welfare?

He ushers me forward into the elevator. "You hurt? Or just scared?"

Every bit of my body trembles. "I'm okay." I sound sullen. I position myself as far away from him as possible, folding my arms across my chest.

Tony frowns at me. The elevator zooms down. "Boss isn't himself. He didn't—" The frown deepens. "Did he force you?"

Okay, that's kinda sweet. This guy really is checking

up on me. But he works for Tacone, head of the crime family, so I'm not sure why he's even asking. "What would you do if I said *yes?*"

Dark fury comes over the guy's face. He takes a step forward toward me. "Is that what happened?" Danger tinges the edges of his voice.

I shake my head. "No. Not like you're thinking." I look away. "Not that. Something else." I don't look, but I can feel his glower still resting on me.

"What would you have done if I said yes?" I ask again. I suppose my morbid curiosity about all things mafia prompts the repeated question.

He presses his lips together and resumes a soldier-like stance. His signal that he's not going to answer.

When the elevator dings open, I dart forward, weaving into the throng of gamblers. Somehow, he stays right behind me. The meat-like hand drops on my nape again. "Slow down. I have orders to take you home."

"I don't need a ride. I'm going to take the bus—really."

He doesn't remove his hand, but uses it to direct me through the crowd, which parts for his big frame and bigger presence. "I'm not gonna whack you, if that's what you think."

I shake my head. I can't believe we're even having a conversation where *whacking* someone is involved.

"Good to know." It's all I seem capable of saying.

He takes me to another elevator—a private one he uses his keycard to get into. We arrive at the lowest floor, which appears to be the private parking area. He leads me to a limousine and opens the back door for me.

"We're going in this?" Maybe he really isn't going to

kill me. I look around at the other cars there. Limos, Bentleys, Porsches, Ferraris. Row after row of luxury cars packed the floor. *Wow.*

Tony smiles like he thinks I'm cute. "Yeah. Get in."

"You're as bossy as your boss," I mutter and he grins.

I do as I'm told. I'm still not a hundred percent sure if this is a death sentence or not, but I can breathe more steadily now.

He doesn't ask for my address but he drives straight to Corey's place and pulls up along the sidewalk in front of the townhouse. A chill runs up my spine.

Tacone had certainly checked up on me. Is this another way he throws his weight around? Showing me he knows where I live and how to find me?

Or is this really a courtesy drop off?

I push the door open the second the car stops.

"Hold up." Tony's deep voice doesn't have the same effect as Tacone's. I don't freeze. Instead, I run for the door. "I said, hold up," he shouts, and I hear the slam of his door. "Mr. Tacone wanted me to give you something."

Hopefully not a bullet between the eyes. I fumble for my keys.

No, I'm being stupid. He drove me home. The guy isn't going to kill me. I turn around and watch him jog up the walk. He pulls the envelope Tacone handed him out of his jacket pocket and gives it to me. My name scrawls across the front in a thin, neat print. For some reason, I'm surprised at how beautiful Tacone's handwriting is.

I draw a shaky breath. "Is that it?"

Tony's eyes crinkle. "Yeah, that's it."

I swallow. "'Kay. Thanks."

He smirks and turns away without another word.

My hands shake as I work the key into the lock.

It's over. A bad day, nothing more. I never have to go back there again. Yes, they know where I live, but they took me home safe and sound. Nothing more will come of this. I had my little taste of the mafia, just like I wanted. Tomorrow I'll start applying for a normal job. One that doesn't involve shady underground characters with huge, hot hands and piercing dark eyes. One without guns, or the jingle of coins in slot machines.

One without Tacone.

Sondra

DEAN, Corey's boyfriend, sits on the couch watching TV. "Hey, Sondra." He looks a little too happy to see me.

My stomach clenches, awareness of my pantyless state increasing. The guy has a habit of leering at me, and I'm afraid he'll somehow figure out there's nothing under my very short dress.

"Hey," I mutter.

He gives me an up and down sweep of his eyes, lingering way too long on my breasts. "What's up?"

There's no way in hell I'm going to tell him about my crazy day. Corey, yes, but not him. Unfortunately, I don't have my own room—I crashed on their couch—so there was nowhere for me to hide. Earning enough to put the deposit on my own place is my first priority, even over getting a car that runs.

I go to my suitcase in the corner and grab a change of clothes before locking myself in the bathroom. Only then do I realize I still clutch the envelope from Mr. Tacone. I stick my thumb under the flap and tear it open. Six crisp hundred-dollar bills slide out with a note of paper.

I draw in my breath. For someone who has pretty much been broke, eating nothing but ramen noodles through college and grad school, it's a lot of money. I had scholarships and assistantships in college, but that still put me below the poverty level. Adjunct teaching hasn't exactly paid the bills, either.

The note's written in the same neat penmanship on the envelope.

SONDRA—

SORRY FOR SCARING YOU. Money doesn't fix everything, but sometimes it helps. I hope you'll return to work tomorrow.

—Nico

MY HEART SKITTERS. *Nico.* He signed his first name? And apologized. Not in person, but still, it's an apology.
I hope you'll return to work tomorrow.

The image of his face leaning just inches from mine as he gripped the towel that bound me against him flashes through in my mind. My knees go weak. He *wants* me to return?

He guessed correctly that I planned to quit and never set foot in the place again. I fan myself with the six hundred-dollar bills. Some people would take a high moral ground. Say they wouldn't let him buy their silence or compliance or whatever. But not me. He's right. Money does go a helluva long way to fixing things.

Still, the asshole held a gun to my head. And stripped me naked. And I *peed.* It was the most humiliating moment of my entire life.

But my sense of violation fades as I remember the way he also shoved me in the shower, toweled me off and murmured, *you're okay.*

I stare at the money. Six hundred dollars closer to moving off my cousin's couch and into my own place. Six hundred dollars closer to getting another car. I can buy groceries and pay my cousin back for what she's already spotted me.

Maybe it wouldn't kill me to show up at work tomorrow. Yes, it had been utterly humiliating, but I'll probably never see the guy again. It would save me the trouble of finding a new interim job while I figure my life out.

I exhale slowly, trying to erase the vision of Tacone brushing my hair back from my face, his penetrating stare. I won't have to see him again. And that's a good thing. Definitely a good thing.

Nico

SONDRA SIMONSON. It's her real name. I asked security to pull everything they can find on her and bring me the file. Along with the video feed of our interaction.

Turns out Samuel, the head of housekeeping, already fired Marissa, Sondra's boss, for leaving her up in my suite, but I call him myself to say it's all right.

And to request Sondra replace the regular penthouse suite housekeeper.

Because if she doesn't quit, I definitely want her up in my room again.

Naked.

Preferably naked and willing this time, but I'd be a goddamn liar if I said I didn't like her a little scared. There was something so appealing about the way she both trembled and got turned on when I stripped her.

Or had I imagined it?

I'll find out soon enough. Where is that damn video feed? I'm like a junkie waiting for his next hit. I can't wait to watch the video of her. I'm going to be fucking my hand all night to the sight of her pouty lips and wide blue eyes decorating my screen.

A knock sounds on the door. "It's Tony." The deep voice of my right-hand man echoes through the door.

"Yeah?"

"I dropped her off." He steps in and gives me a careful look. I know he didn't come in here just to tell me that. He came in to find out what the hell happened. Why I sent the maid home wet and scared.

31

He's worried about me. My mental state is starting to crumble with the inability to sleep. He's too smart to come out and ask me what happened. He knows I'd tell him to mind his own fucking business. But he's made a career out of standing around me silently, serving as my bodyguard, making himself available when I do feel like confiding.

He's not family. He's not even Italian. He's just a big, loyal guy from Cicero who decided I was the guy he was going to follow into the bowels of hell. I guess you could say he's the closest thing I have to a friend.

If a Tacone ever really has a friend.

"She's new. I thought she looked off, so I strip searched her."

A muscle in Tony's jaw tightens but he doesn't say anything. Tony is absolutely a defender of women. His ma was abused by his dad pretty bad and he's still eager to even that score with any guy who manhandles a woman. Probably even, if it came down to it, me.

But I don't usually make a habit out of mistreating women.

This one was a special case.

I purse my lips and shrug. "I also may have pointed a gun at her head while I was questioning her." I tell him in case there's some mess we need to clean up from the fallout. Hopefully Sondra won't kick up a fuss. I don't think she will.

And for some reason that bugs the hell out of me.

I have terrible taste in men.

Smart, well-educated, smoking hot little number like

her shouldn't be walking around with that fatal flaw that puts her in danger. Especially not in Vegas.

Except it's probably that terrible taste that turned her supple and pliant in my arms, too. Those incredible nipples pebbled up, that pussy turned wet for me. And I hadn't even been coming on to her. I was rough-handling her like a deranged lunatic.

Fuck.

Tony shoves his hands in his pockets. "Jesus, Nico. The lack of sleep has you paranoid."

"I know." I run my hand through my hair.

"You need to take something. Have you tried the drugs?"

I have a whole shelfful of pharmaceuticals that are supposed to help me sleep, but either they don't work or I don't like the way they make me feel afterward. Not that I like the delirium I'm under now. "Nah. I think I'll be able to sleep tonight."

"That's what you said last night."

I look out the wall of windows that make up my penthouse suite. "So you got her home? Was she okay?"

"She was skittish. You pay her off?"

The words *pay her off* set my teeth on edge, even though that's exactly what I did. Still, it sounds so sordid when associated with her. It's the same reason I don't want to see her dealing on my floor. She shouldn't be sullied by all the shit that goes down at this hotel casino.

She shouldn't be sullied by me.

Too bad I want to dirty her in every possible way.

If I were a better man, I would make certain our paths

never cross again. But I'm not. I'm not a good man. I put her right back in the lion's den.

I'll have to wait until tomorrow to see if she's as smart she looks and she vows to never set foot in this place again.

~

Sondra

I TAKE a shower and exit the bathroom, unsurprised to find Dean lurking just outside it, ostensibly in the kitchen. I haven't figured out how to tell Corey I think her boyfriend's a lecherous, no-good cheating asshole. I don't have any proof—just the way he looks at me, and seems way more interested in talking to me or hanging out when we're alone.

Considering I'm a magnet for cheating boyfriends, I know the vibe.

I usually make it a habit not to be around when Dean is at the townhouse without Corey, but Tacone's guy drove me home too quickly. I try to make the best of it. "Hey, Dean. You feel like driving me to the grocery store? I got paid today." *For getting strip searched.*

This time when the memory of Mr. Tacone's—Nico's —large hot hands roaming over my body flashed back, the fear is gone. A brief fantasy flickers in my mind—him peeling my panties down my legs for a different reason...

You know how much a guy like me would spend for a night with a girl like you?

Five thousand dollars!

Stop thinking about him!

I need to forget Nico Tacone is exactly the kind of man who makes my toes curl. Dark. Dangerous. Unpredictable. The ultimate bad boy.

Yes, I'm in danger of falling to the dark side again. Big time.

I need to stay strong.

Corey's boyfriend sighs and rolls his eyes—apparently it's a huge inconvenience to give me a ride to the store. He's been generally insinuating how much I owe them since the day I showed up. "Yeah, okay, I'll take you." He's probably just disappointed we aren't going to be alone together at the townhouse.

I don't care about Lame-o's reaction to having me crash at their place. Corey and I are practically sisters. We grew up in small-town Michigan, cousins living across the street from each other. Her dad's in law enforcement and he was an abusive asshole before he walked out on her mom, so she spent most of her time at my place.

But a guy has never come between us before, and Dean seems like the type of guy to create any number of dramas. I need to get out of here before things get even more awkward. Yet another reason to go to work tomorrow.

CHAPTER 3

 *ondra*

"WHAT IN THE HELL HAPPENED YESTERDAY?" My boss, Marissa, demands the minute I show up in the housekeeping area.

I try to keep my face blank. I don't know how much she knows, but I sure as hell don't want the whole staff hearing I got stripped down to my panties in Mr. Tacone's bathroom. Or that he paid me six hundred cash for it. Or that two dozen peach roses arrived for me at Corey's townhouse last night.

I've never been given two dozen roses in my life. I gave half of them to Corey, who dragged me into her bedroom to tell her what happened in private. Corey found the story insane and declared Tacone has a thing for me.

I lift my eyes to my supervisor's. "What happened with your son?" I attempt to redirect the conversation.

She isn't having it. She waves her hand with impatience. "Concussion. He fell backward onto concrete in the schoolyard. What happened with you?"

My face heats. I open my mouth but I'm not really sure how to answer. "What did you hear?"

Irritation flashes across her face. "Well, first Samuel called to say I was fired for allowing you up there. Then he called back to say no, actually, he heard from Nico Tacone himself and everything was fine. So fine, in fact, Tacone requested you be the regular penthouse cleaning person. *Which pays double what you're making now.*" She folds her arms across her chest. "So what happened?"

Wait...what? My heart takes off running ahead of me. *He wants me to be his regular cleaning person?* That would mean seeing him again—face to face. The man who humiliated me and ogled my naked body. Who's seen me crying. And wet. No. I can't.

But double the pay...that would definitely get me out of Corey's place faster. Out of Vegas, if that's what I decide.

Marissa stands there, eyebrows raised, waiting for an explanation. I opt for a partial truth. "While I was cleaning Nico Tacone's room, he returned and freaked out because he didn't know me. I mean *freaked out.* He held a gun to my head."

Marissa slaps a hand over her mouth and her eyes get wide.

"I seriously thought I was going to die."

Sympathy washes over her features. "Oh my God, Sondra, I'm so sorry. I never should have left you there alone."

38

I shrug. "It ended up okay. Once he checked out my story, I think he felt bad about scaring the shit out of me." *Or pee, as the case may be.* "He sent me home in a limo with his driver."

Marissa lets out a surprised gust of laughter. "No. *Way.*"

I nod. "True story."

"Well, it probably doesn't hurt that you're young and beautiful. I'm sure if it were me, I'd have been fired on the spot."

"You're young and beautiful."

She smiles. "Flattery will get you everywhere."

I try not to let her words feed the stupid thrill already buzzing beneath all my more sane thoughts. Is Nico taken by me? I shouldn't hope so. Surely my better sense will kick in soon. Except I didn't sleep last night. I had my fingers between my legs, fantasizing about what it would've been like if Nico Tacone turned me to face the counter in his bathroom and plunged his authoritative cock inside me until I screamed.

Suddenly Marissa's brows slam back down. "Do you feel safe?" she demands. "Because I'm not going to send a vulnerable young woman in there to get molested. Was that the vibe you got from him?"

Was it? No. Not really. Other than the almost kissing me part. And sending me roses. But *molested* is a strong word. I didn't feel *that* vulnerable. Yes, he terrified me, but he also fascinated. He actually took care of me in a weird way—shoving me in that shower to clean up and drying me off. And taking off my soaked panties.

But do I feel safe?

39

No.

Is that half the appeal? Corey would say yes. Because I possess some aberrant thrill-seeking gene when it comes to men.

"Yeah, he's okay. I don't get a creepy vibe from him," I mutter, stacking my cart with supplies.

"Are you sure? Because if you're still too shaken up, I'm not afraid to tell them. They've got a human resource nightmare waiting to happen with you."

Somehow I doubt the Tacone family gives a shit about human resource problems. They probably have their own special way of dealing with problems that don't involve lawsuits or payouts. Unless you count the payout Nico gave me yesterday of six hundred crisp ones.

"Yeah, I'm sure. I'll be fine."

"Okay, here's your new keycard. You're in charge of the three suites on the top floor and nothing else, according to Mr. Tacone."

"That won't take all day, though. What do I do when I'm done?"

"You get to go home."

Oh—so I'm really not getting a raise. Well, I'll be working fewer hours for the same amount of money, so it's an improvement. But it doesn't get me out of Corey's house any sooner. Still, I'm not complaining. It will give me time to apply for teaching positions.

I take my cart and the new keycard she gives me into the elevator. On the top floor, I clean the other two suites first. They both have two bedrooms. I wonder who they belong to—Nico's brothers? Cousins? I wish I knew more about the operation here. When I first applied at the

Bellissimo and Corey told me it was mafia run, I Googled it, but nothing came up. Zero. Not that I'm surprised. If Nico Tacone assumes a new maid is bugging his place, then he's either paranoid, or he has some serious secrets to keep hidden. The second thought sends a shiver running up my spine.

Curiosity killed the cat, Sondra. Yeah. Too bad the attraction to the wrong sort of men never fades for me.

After I finish with the other two suites, I knock on Nico's door. I have to admit, my heart beats faster as I stand there listening for an answer. I'm both thrilled and quaking at the idea of seeing him again.

I use the keycard and enter. I hear his voice first, then catch sight of him pacing out on his balcony, talking—actually, yelling—into his phone. His head jerks up and eyes lock on me with the same dark intensity they wore yesterday. He says something more into the phone and then drops it into his pocket, never taking his gaze from me.

I push the cart into the center of the room, hoping I'm hiding how much he unnerves me.

He slides open the glass door from the balcony and stalks toward me. "You came back."

Does he sound pleased, or am I imagining it?

"Yeah," I mumble and make a big show out of pulling supplies from the cart.

"I wasn't sure you would."

I turn around and yelp to find him right in front of me, the heat of his body radiating into mine.

Oh lord, he's still beautiful. Chocolate brown eyes with long dark, curling lashes—the kind a woman would kill for. Olive skin. His square jaw sports a five-o'clock shadow. The bags under his eyes are still there, but not quite as pronounced today. His periwinkle blue button-down gapes at the collar, revealing a light dusting of dark curls.

I run my tongue over my lips to moisten them and his eyes follow the movement. "Are you going to strip search me again?"

His lips kick up at the corners and suddenly I find myself crowded against the cart. He's not quite touching me, but it wouldn't take much to bring our bodies flush with each other. "Do you want me to?"

Yes.

"No, thanks, I'm good." I swallow, heat pooling between my legs, my core quivering. His lips are just inches away. I can smell his breath—minty and fresh. "Did you sleep last night?"

He arches a brow—yes, just one. It's movie star sexy. "Are you asking after my well-being, *bambina*? After what I did to you yesterday?"

My face grows warm at the reminder and I shrug.

"You're as sweet as you look, aren't you?" His face darkens and he takes a step back. "You shouldn't have come." He shakes his head. "I figured you'd quit for sure."

Suddenly I'm suffocating under his disappointment in me, which mirrors my own. When will I ever smarten up? Bartenders who like to drop ecstasy and mafioso casino owners are bad news.

As if he senses my change in mood, he reaches out and touches my shoulder. It's a light touch—respectful.

Nothing sexy or dominating about it. "I'm sorry about yesterday, Sondra."

The way he says my name makes my insides twist and wriggle. I didn't expect it to sound so... *familiar* on his lips.

"I'm glad you came back—even though I wish to hell, for your sake, you didn't."

I shove my chin forward. "So which is it? You want me here or you don't?"

Suddenly I'm trapped against the cart, caged by the two steel bands of his arms. Tacone comes flush up against me, hard, muscular lines pressed against my curves. His cock bulges at my stomach. "I jerked off three times watching our video last night, *bambina*." His voice comes as a hoarse rumble that enters my body.

My pussy squeezes, thrills of shock rippling through me.

What video? Oh dear lord, did his security surveillance catch the whole interaction? Who else has seen it?

"I was so sure you were a plant yesterday because there's something special about you. Something that hooks me right here." He curls his finger in front of his solar plexus. "So yeah. I wanted to see you again. Wanted to hear your voice. Make sure you're okay." He drops one of his hands to my hip.

I suck my lower lip in between my teeth. I'm trembling almost as much as I did yesterday, only this time, there's no fear. Just excitement.

Desire.

His palm slides around my hip to cup my ass. I put my hands up on his chest, ready to push him away, but I don't follow through. The thread of indignation running through me is drowned out by his velvety voice.

He cants his head, studying me. "Beautiful face. Perfect tits, that lush little body of yours. I've seen that before. But the way that sweet pussy got wet even though I scared the hell out of you. The way you revealed everything, like you really have nothing to hide..."

Oh gawd.

My *sweet pussy* is definitely wet again, clenching and releasing as his hot breath caresses my cheek.

"Have you forgiven me?" His voice drops to an intimate level.

Another squeeze of my lady parts tells me I'm already lost.

I want to say *no* because of the humiliation I endured, but, once more, my body betrays me—he has me leaning toward him, panting, hungry. "Not yet," is as close I can get to a negative.

He brushes my cheek with the backs of his fingers. I get the feeling he's testing to see if I'll resist.

I don't.

Score another one for the bad boy.

"Just like that," he whispers, staring down at me. "That's the look."

What look?

One corner of his mouth lifts and he cups the back of my head, pulling my face up to his. "I'm not sorry."

My eyes widen and I try to jerk away, but he holds me fast, and goes on like I didn't react. "I wouldn't have missed that encounter for all the world." His lips descend on mine, firm and demanding.

A wave of lust rolls over me. I melt into him, parting my lips, allowing his tongue to sweep into my mouth. Heat explodes in every cell of my body.

He pulls away, nostrils flaring. "As sweet as I imagined." He licks his lips, as if tasting me. "*That* I regretted. Not tasting you."

I lick my lips, too. "I didn't say you could kiss me." The breathy quality of my voice belies my reaction.

He gives a harsh laugh. "No, you didn't. I stole that kiss." His features harden. "That's why you shouldn't have come back. You stick around here, *piccolina*, and I'm going to make you sorry. Probably make us both sorry." He steps back and surveys me. "Or maybe not. I might just take what I want without apology."

My pulse skitters. My panties are damp with arousal, nipples chafe against my bra. I'm one part scared, two parts turned on. And damn, if his warning doesn't make me want to offer myself up to him on a silver platter.

He straightens his jacket and walks toward the door. "So I'm going to leave, *amore*. You do your thing here." He stops at the door and turns back to face me. "And you'd better think about what you want to tell me next time. Make up your mind. Yes or no. And I'll make up mine. But I'm warning you, *bambi*—you have even a little bit of *yes* mixed in with your *no*, I'm going to mow you down to the ground." He points a warning finger at me. "Believe it."

When he leaves, I have to hang onto the housekeeping cart to keep my legs under me.

What. In the hell. Just happened?

I want to call Corey and report, because today's story turned out almost as exciting as yesterday's, but I don't dare. Tacone has cameras everywhere, and he already confessed to jerking off to the footage of me yesterday. I wouldn't be surprised if he reviewed today's feed, too. And I really need to get my head straight before I open my mouth around him again.

Because he just gave me an ultimatum. Make up my mind. I don't know the full implications of that decision or even what it entails, but I do know one thing—

There's way too much *yes* in me to say *no*.

~

Nico

I HEAD down to the main floor.

There are about a hundred reasons why I shouldn't fuck around with the hot little art historian housekeeper, but none of them make it easy for me to walk out the door when she's still in my suite.

I'm going to have to make sure I'm not there when she cleans. Hell, if I had any decency in me whatsoever, I'd call her boss and have her transferred back to the main floors right now. I wait a few moments to see if my moral compass takes over enough to follow through on that thought.

Sadly, it doesn't.

Sondra, Sondra, Sondra. I'll have to hope her good sense kicks in.

It's funny; the only other time I had it so bad for a girl was when I was twelve and became obsessed with my brother's girlfriend, Trinidad Winters. But that was just my pubescent lust kicking into high gear. Trini was always around, riding along in the car when Gio picked me up, watching movies on our couch in miniskirts that rode up her long legs.

Sondra is nothing like Trini. She's nothing like Jenna, the mafia princess I'm supposed to marry. I don't date, but she's definitely not like any of the girls I fuck—paid or volunteer.

I want more of her. I love the way she got breathless and excited back there. It wouldn't have taken much for me to pry those knees apart and show her just how bad her taste in men really runs.

Oh, I'd have her screaming. Pleasuring Sondra would be easy—the girl looks ready to go off like a firecracker. Hell, I'd keep her up all night moaning my name and I wouldn't even miss the sleep.

I walk around the tables, scanning for Sondra's cousin, Corey. Just to get a look at her. Not because I'm totally obsessed with this girl and need to know everything about her. Researching her full background was necessary. I had to make completely sure she's not working some angle.

The Tacones have a lot of enemies. Hell, I probably have enemies within the Tacone family. I run my Vegas branch of the business on the up and up, but there's a long history of violence and crime going back at least three generations to the Chicago underground. And then there are the enemies from the legitimate business world. Anyone might send in a femme fatale to get close to me, learn my secrets and set me up to fall.

And Sondra Simonson is exactly the kind of girl they'd send.

No, that's bullshit.

She's not. She's nothing like a professional. But if my enemies were really smart, if they could somehow intuit what's taken me by surprise, they'd send Sondra Simonson to take me down.

Because it's for certain.

I'm not going to be able to stop myself from going after her.

I find Corey working a blackjack table. I see the resemblance. She's as lovely as Sondra, but totally not my type. Tall, red-haired. Leggy. She looks sophisticated and sharp. Deals fast and clean. Appears to be a good asset to my casino.

She's focused on her customers and yet her gaze flicks around the room, taking in everything. Including me. Next time she glances up, she skips the room-sweep and looks straight at me. I saunter over to her table.

Nothing shows on her face, but I know she's aware of who I am. Wonders what I'm doing at her table. My presence must make the customers nervous, because after a few hands, the table clears out.

"Mr. Tacone," she murmurs without quite meeting my eye. She's properly deferential. Plays it just right.

I shove my hands in my pockets. I'm not even sure what I want from her. Some more information about Sondra, I suppose.

When I don't say anything, she offers, "You scared my cousin yesterday."

I nod. "Yeah."

She narrows her eyes at me. "You don't still think you need to worry about her, do you?"

"No." I scrub a hand across my face. "Scale of one to ten—how traumatized was she?"

Corey has an excellent poker face. Nothing shows—not surprise, not anger. Nothing. "Eight. But the flowers and money helped." Corey moves in for the kill. "A dealer job would help her even more."

I shake my head. "Not gonna happen."

She lowers her gaze to her cards without comment, spreading them out on the table and flipping them over back and forth in a perfect ripple, showing off her tricks. After a long moment, she says, "If you weren't my boss, I'd tell you to stay away from her."

I like her pluck.

I pull a fifty-dollar chip from my pocket and drop it on the table for her as a tip. "I can't."

CHAPTER 4

ondra

COREY and I ride into work together the following week. I love when we work the same shift, but she hates it, because it means she's working days, and she makes more money at night.

It's the first chance I've had to fill her in on the latest with Tacone, which is nothing.

"So you haven't seen him since the day he kissed you?"

"Nope. The next day I went in and there was a fifty on the table. I left it. The day after that, he left a hundred-dollar bill with my name on it."

"You took it, of course."

I didn't want to. I was afraid it would mean something. Like if I accept his money, I'll owe him something later. Except I really can use the money. I need at least two thousand for a deposit and first month's rent. And another three thousand to buy a car that runs.

"Yeah. And then he left another one a couple days later." I dig them out of my purse and hand it to her. "Here."

She shoves my hand away. "What's that for?"

"To go toward my share of the rent."

She rolls her eyes. "Save it. Then you can move out sooner." She gives me a teasing grin.

"You sick of having me?"

"No, I love it, actually. But I think Dean's tired of sharing the family room. He likes watching movies at night, you know."

Yeah, I noticed. Dean hasn't exactly stopped that habit even though the sofa's my bed. He stays up watching until one in the morning most every night.

"And every time we have sex, I cringe because the walls are paper thin. Can you hear?"

I make a face. "Yeah, sometimes." They have sex at least once a day, sometimes more. I swear, Dean's a sex addict. Not that once a day is bad, but I don't see why he's looking at me when he gets plenty from Corey.

"I think he wants to have a threesome."

"Ew. Corey!"

She laughs. "I told him no way. I don't share. Ever. Not even with my best cousin who's like a sister."

Thank God.

What in the hell would I say if she was into it?

But yeah, gross. Apparently my instincts are right about Dean.

"So back to Nico Tacone. What's going to happen when you do see him again?"

Er...how should I know?

"I mean, you need to decide. I think the guy has the hots for you. And his instinct is to exploit you, like he probably exploits all women, but something made him hold back."

"He thinks I'm *innocent* or something." I say *innocent* like it's a dirty word.

Corey grins at me. She knows better. "There's something about you that comes off that way. I used to hate you for it."

I gape. "What?"

She shrugs. "When we were kids. I mean, my dad was such a prick and I didn't trust anyone as far as I could throw them, but you were so pure. With you, what you see is what you get. It's what makes you trust losers. But it's a pretty amazing quality."

I roll my eyes. "Great. An amazing quality that made you hate me as a kid and makes me date losers. Sounds like one I should keep."

Her eyes slide over at me. "No, really. I hope you never lose it."

She sounds so serious I shut up.

"Anyway, I think that's what he's reacting to. You're out of place in Vegas." Corey pulls into the Bellissimo's drive and heads toward the back employee lot. "So how's it going to go when you see him?"

I draw a breath. I want to lie and say I hope I won't see him at all, but Corey already knows the truth. I shrug. "I'll follow his lead."

Corey parks and faces me. "Seriously? How's that been working out for you so far?"

"I know, I know, but…" But it's part of the fascination. The way he dominates every moment we're together makes my knees weak.

We get out of the car and walk into the casino together through the service entrance.

"I think you should decide. If you want to go for him, make a play. If not, be professional. Don't let him jerk you around again. Okay?"

I nod, but I'm not sure about anything. I need to quit this job. Soon. Before I humiliate myself even more.

My phone buzzes as I walk down the hall. It's a friend from Reno. She wrote, *Tanner stopped by. Seemed really heartbroken. He begged me for your new number. I told him to get lost.*

Right. Heartbroken. Ha. He wants the car back.

Thanks, I text back. I definitely don't want to hear from him.

I head to the employee locker room to change into my pink housekeeping dress. Like every day this week, there's an uptick in excitement as I put it on, remembering how Tacone stripped me out of it.

Damn. I have it bad for this guy and he'd be my worst man-move yet.

Nico

. . .

"The fuck you are," I snarl at my oldest brother, Junior, through the phone. He's just informed me he's sending ten guys to Vegas to take over the cocaine scene here.

"You wanna try that again?"

"We had an agreement. I keep things on the up and up here so your money can be laundered through. I do not need the Vegas police or the Feds breathing down my neck because you want to increase your share of street drug sales. It's not worth it."

"I decide what's worth it and what's not."

I go silent with my disagreement. Junior doesn't run the outfit. Our father is boss, but he's currently sitting in a federal prison for four more years on a tax fraud charge.

"No, Junior," I say after the pause. "I have enough to deal with here. I know this city. I know the cops. I know the mayor. The risk does not outweigh the reward."

"Maybe you need me to come help you run your business better, then."

"Fuck you." I squeeze my eyes shut, because I really shouldn't talk to my brother that way, and if I don't de-escalate things, I'm going to be pulling my balls out of my ass. "Listen, J—I'm sorry. That was disrespectful. I didn't mean it."

Junior makes a sound in his throat.

"You're happy with the way I run things here, right? I make *La Famiglia* a lot of money, no?" There can be no doubt of his answer. I make four times what all their illegal operations make in Chicago, and everything I do here is on the up and up.

He makes another affirmative sound.

55

"So please trust me on this. I'm sorry I was being a prick. I get too used to being my own bossman here. But I know what's gonna work in my city. Cocaine dealing is too risky. Too dominated by the Latin American gangs. And it could threaten everything I have going here, ah?"

"You're being a pussy."

I have to work to keep my temper in check. I don't dignify his taunt with an answer.

Junior waits another moment, then he says, "We'll talk about it when I come out there."

I stiffen. "When is that?"

"Next week. Ma wants to move out for the winter. Says she misses you too much. I figure I'll come along and find her a house."

I'm about to snap that *I* can find her a house, but I manage to put a cork in it. He wants to come here and throw around his weight. I'd better get my head on straight before he gets here. Keeping his shit out of Vegas is my number one priority.

Sondra

I TAKE the elevator up to the top floor. Something makes me try Tacone's room first—some sixth sense he'll be there this time. I knock on the door, but hear nothing. So much for intuition.

I key myself in and get to work.

It's empty, as it's been the past week. A crisp fifty dollar bill lays on the table with a note and my name. At this rate, I'll earn enough to move out of Corey's by the end of the month.

Which, considering what she told me about Dean's interest in a threesome, is even more necessary.

I leave the bill on the table until I finish. It's for a job well-done and I'll make damn sure I do my best before I take the money. I clean the bathrooms and bedroom and head into the study. I end up in the office last. Because Marissa was paranoid about it, I stay way the hell away from the desk, dusting the book cases, emptying the trash and vacuuming. Noticing a spider web in the upper corner of the window, I grab the broom to swipe it. And that's when the other end of the broom knocks over something on Tacone's desk.

I jump and whirl to see coffee spilling across the papers.

Oh shit.

Crap, crap, crap.

I run for my rags, and come back, mopping things up as fast as I can. But it's too late. Half the papers on his desk are soaking wet, stained brown.

What should I do?

I separate them and lay them out individually to dry, trying not to look at the contents. I'm not supposed to be seeing this stuff.

"What the fuck?"

A little shriek leaves my lips and I knock the now-empty coffee mug over again.

Tacone looms in the doorway, his hulk more

menacing than ever. His eyes glitter black, a muscle jumps in his jaw.

"Oh God..." I right the coffee mug again. "I'm so sorry. I knocked over your coffee and got it all over everything. I know we're not supposed to touch the desks—I definitely didn't plan to, but..."

Tacone walks closer, suspicious eyes sweeping the desk, the floor, my body, the room. He still has bags under his eyes like he hasn't been sleeping.

"I didn't look at anything—I swear."

In a flash, he wraps his large hand around my throat from behind, loosely cupping the front of my neck. He pulls me back, so my ass bumps into his legs. "What did you see?" His voice is low and dangerous, but the hand on my neck is more a caress than a threat, especially when his thumb strokes lightly along my pulse.

I close my eyes. "Nothing," I croak. "I saw nothing. I swear."

"Nosiness won't be forgiven, Sondra." His voice is pure sex. Total seduction. His breath feathers hot across my ear. The hard muscles of his body press against my softer form. "Are you telling me the truth?"

"Yes." It comes out as a half-moan, half-gasp, but not because I'm scared. I'm totally turned on.

Tacone's other arm snakes around my waist. His hand splays flat across my belly, inching down. "Your only sin is clumsiness?"

"Yes, sir."

He likes that I call him *sir*. I don't know how I can tell, but I know he does.

Zingers of electricity run through my body, lighting it

up from the inside, and I swear I sense the answering charge from his cells. My panties are beyond damp—they're soaked.

"I guess that only calls for a little *correction*." He nips my ear.

My heart thuds, probably so hard he can feel it through my back.

"Put your hands on the desk."

My belly flips. Oh my lord, is he going to spank me? A shiver runs through me. He's excited too. His cock presses into my back, and his breath rasps in and out as fast as mine. He releases me and steps back and I obey, bending to rest my palms flat on the desk in front of me.

I hear a deep rumble of approval behind me. His two hands grip my hips and he pulls, angling my butt even further back. He slowly slides his hands down the fabric of my skirt, caressing my curves before he releases me. "I'll let you keep your uniform on." His voice is impossibly deep. "Only because this time, if I take that zipper down again, I won't hold back."

The floor tilts and a wave of dizziness floods through me and then I slam back to reality when his palm crashes down on my ass.

Smack.

I gasp and list to the side automatically, but then I put myself back in position. I hold still for his punishment.

"Mm. I *knew* this ass would be spankable," he rumbles.

He slaps the other cheek. *Hard.* I have to close my lips against the squeak that rises in my throat. Another slap, and another. It's a little too much, but just when I'm about to protest, he starts rubbing my offended cheeks, massaging away the sting.

I pant, my pussy clenching, heart tapping out a rapid beat.

Tacone strokes down my hip until he reaches bare thigh. He starts to slide up my leg, under the uniform skirt, then stops, and pulls my dress hem lower. "You'd better get back to work before I take this way too far."

Uhhh...what? I'm way too horned up to just pull my dress down and get back to work. In fact, the very idea of it pisses me off. If a female could get blue balls, I'd have them. My clit throbs, my nipples are hard, sensitive points.

I lift my torso and whirl around to confront him. Before I can speak, he catches me at the nape and holds me captive for a kiss. Hard lips twist over mine with a bruising intensity. He sucks my lower lip into his mouth, nips it. His tongue sweeps between my lips.

I mewl and kiss him back, grateful for the desk supporting my ass, or I would fall down.

"*Bellissima*," he murmurs when he pulls away. "I can't seem to keep my hands off you."

No need, my wanton inner slut moans.

But with a pained look, he releases me and steps back. "Go on." He turns me and smacks my ass in dismissal.

A storm of emotions flood through me—humiliation mingling with lust and turning into white hot anger.

Okay. He wants to toy with me?

Fine.

Two can play at this game.

~

Nico

I SIT DOWN at my desk and try not to watch the very turned on, angry woman strutting through my suite.

It seems I'm destined to be inappropriate with Sondra Simonson. Keeping my hands off her is an impossibility. I tried to stay away—*Madonna,* I did. But here she is, surrendering to me again with that same scared-but-turned on vibe that drives me crazy.

I never paid much attention to my thing for dominating women.

Oh, I like to be in charge—no doubt about that. But that just means I call the shots. It's why I normally use professionals who do as I say without question. But none of them ever tremble and gasp like Sondra. None of them have had a genuine response to me. None of them flash that fury she just did for not following through.

If she only knew I'm trying to do a kindness by releasing her. I shouldn't have spanked her in the first place.

But that ass!

That juicy, spankable ass.

And the adorable little sounds she made when I smacked it.

I give my cock a hard squeeze through my trousers and watch Sondra's hips sway as she sashays past my door with a dust cloth. Her lips are swollen from our kiss. I still taste the sweetness of her on mine. Like strawberries and green tea. I want to taste her everywhere.

It was all I could do not to pull out my cock and give it to her hard and fast right here, over my desk. That will teach her not to spill coffee on my papers.

Fuck. I'm losing my mind.

One small part of me still worries she's not legit. But she has to be. I researched the hell out of her. By all appearances, she's an innocent, middle-class beauty from Marshall, Michigan. She was a straight A student who graduated *magna cum laude* from a small, private liberal arts college, and then went on to get a Master's degree in art history from the University of Wisconsin. Her parents still live across the street from her cousin Corey's mom. Now, Corey's dad is a fed. That came out when we hired her. But she appears to be estranged. And she's worked for us for almost a year without any suspicious behavior.

I couldn't unearth a single lie or reason for concern about Sondra, unless I count her ex-boyfriend, who appears to be a small-time ecstasy dealer in Reno. But she did say she has bad taste in men.

Sondra positions herself at my bookcase, giving me a front row seat to her backside, which is so lovingly cupped by her uniform dress that I want to send a huge bonus to whoever on my team picked out that particular style.

She wiggles her ass as she flicks the dust cloth across the wood.

Oh God. Is she doing that on purpose?

She bends at the waist to dust the shelf in front of her.

When she drops to her hands and knees and arches her back to dust the lowest one, I'm sure it's all for me.

My control, already a frayed wire, snaps. I surge up from the desk and stalk around to her.

"Is that little show for me, *piccolina*?" I hardly recognize my voice, it's so gravelly.

She looks over her shoulder with mock innocence.

That's what undoes me—those big baby blues blink with total sex kitten appeal.

She's wearing her hair back in a messy bun today and I wrap my hand around it and pull her up to her knees. I'm already on my knees on the floor behind her, but I don't remember getting there. I wrap my arm around the front of her and cup her mons possessively, still forcing her head back against my shoulder.

"Are you trying to drive me crazy, Sondra Simonson?" I rub over her slit and find her panties already damp with arousal. "I don't think you understand what you're about to unleash." My fingers slide under the gusset of her panties to make contact with her wet flesh.

She lets out another of those gasps that drive me insane.

"I understand." I put my lips up against her ear and speak as I rub a slow circle around her swollen clit. "It wasn't fair of me to spank you without giving you a reward, was it?"

She moans.

I screw one finger into her wet channel.

I release her hair and move my hand to slide in the zippered opening of her dress.

She's already shaking and bucking, ready to blow.

"I ought to fuck you until your teeth rattle for getting me so horned up." I curl a second finger into her and pump lightly. "But I suppose I owe you this release, don't I?"

Her pussy is so juicy and responsive, my eyes are rolling back in my head. And that's just from fingering her. I will really lose it if I put my cock in this girl.

"Are you going to let me make up for scaring you the first time we met, *bambina?*"

Her only answer is a breathy moan.

I pull my fingers out of her and swat her pussy. "Are you? Answer me with words, baby."

"Yes!" There's surprise and annoyance in her voice and more than a little desperation. It makes me smile.

"Good girl." I tap her clit. I'm dying to taste her, especially now that I've decided it's my duty to reward her. I let her go and put my hands on her hips, applying a little gentle direction. "Crawl over there to the couch, baby. I need to get these panties off you."

There's zero hesitation. She's totally and completely mine. She obeys without a hint of embarrassment, crawling to the couch, then stopping and turning, probably to see how I want her. Fuck, this girl makes me crazy.

I push her torso down on the seat of the sofa and pull the skirt of her dress up. This is how I wanted her before. Ass bared for her spanking.

I yank her panties down her thighs and she scrambles to kick them off. Only a few red splotches remain from where I slapped her before. I don't hold back. I spank her ass, the loud crack of my hand against her bare flesh echoing through the room. I lay five hard slaps down, then stop and rub.

I can tell by her gasps it hurt, so I lean over and kiss each cheek. "You okay, baby?"

"Um…"

"You want more, or was that enough?"

She's quiet for a moment and I'm suddenly sick to think I took it too far, but then she says in a small voice, "A little more."

"That's my girl." I give her three more, then rub her pink skin. I definitely want to fuck her now. And I mean fuck her in the dirtiest, nastiest way. Like hold her by the hair and bang into her until she screams for mercy.

But I'm not going to.

I promised her a reward, and I intend to give it.

"Sit up on the couch and spread those sexy thighs," I direct.

She scrambles up to comply and I get a good look at her face. Her cheeks are flushed, eyes glazed. Her hair is messy with a just-fucked look. It's a picture I'd love to see every goddamn day for the rest of my life.

But that's not an option.

Rein it in, Nico.

I can't have this girl. I mean, I could. I'm Nico Tacone, owner of The Bellissimo, capo of the Tacone crime family of Chicago. I can take anything I damn well please.

But I *can't.*

Not this girl.

She deserves a real man. Someone she could marry and have art historian babies with. Not a crime boss who's been pledged to another since birth.

I push her knees wide and get an eyeful of that pink heart I've been fantasizing about.

Gotta taste.

I reach my hands under her thighs to palm her ass and pull her closer, right up to my mouth.

The moan she lets out intoxicates me. I take one long, slow lick, parting her labia as I travel upward, toward her clit. She jerks the moment I make contact with it and makes a needy, whining sound.

"Is that where you want me, baby?"

She threads her fingers through my hair. "Y-yes, please."

I flick her clit repeatedly with the tip of my tongue. "So sweet. You taste so good, baby. And you asked so nicely." I flatten my tongue and take another long sweep, then make it pointy and penetrate her. Her juices leak onto my tongue, tangy and slick. I control her pelvis even more, lifting her so I can lick her anus, too.

She squeals, but I hold her thighs apart so she can't clamp them closed, can't get away from the torture of pleasure I want to bestow on her. I nip her labia, suck them. I know I could get her off, quick. She's already gearing to blow, but the longer I hold her off, the bigger her orgasm, and for some reason, I'm feeling competitive, like I want this to be the best fucking orgasm of her life.

Maybe because I know I can't keep her.

And I really want to fucking keep her.

I screw one finger into her while I flick her clit. She wriggles over it, trying to take me deeper. Greedy little thing. I add a second finger, close my lips around her tiny bud and suck.

She screams, but I back off, releasing her clit and pumping my fingers.

"Oh," she pants. "Please. Oh please, oh...N-Nico."

I fucking love that she said my name, even more than I loved when she called me *sir* earlier.

I especially love her moaning my name in that incendiary breathy fuck-me voice. I slow the pumping motion and instead curl my fingers to tickle her inner wall, seeking her G-spot. Her eyes fly wide when I find it, something akin to panic flaring. She writhes her pelvis on the leather couch. I pump my fingers so I hit the G-spot every time and she shrieks, her fingers tearing at my hair.

"That's it, baby. Come for me."

Her juices leak all over my fingers and her pussy squeezes, pulsing her release out in quick flutters. I let her finish, then massage her pussy with my fingers, a slow in and out and around, stirring inside her, then pulling my fingers out and sliding them up and down her slit. She shudders out another release.

She looks beautiful. Her blonde hair fans out around her on the couch, messy and adorable. Her eyes are glazed, lids heavy.

My cock throbs.

But I can't do it.

～

Sondra

NICO STARES at me like a starved animal, appearing

almost pained with desire. He eases his fingers from me and rubs circles on my inner thighs with his thumbs. I'm boneless with the pleasure of my orgasm. Even without intercourse, I have to say it was the best climax I've ever had. Everything about the encounter made it hot, starting with the lead up of Nico strip searching me the day we met, then spanking me, then this. Combine that with Nico's considerable skill and genuine interest in my pleasure, and I'm doubting this sexual experience will ever be beat.

And considering he hasn't been satisfied yet, I don't think it's over.

How much better will it get?

"Th-thank you," I say when my voice returns to me. My throat's sore from crying out, which isn't something I normally do.

Nico's smile seems almost sad. "You're so fucking sweet." His hands roam up to my breasts. He lowers the zipper of my dress and pulls my boobs out of the bra cups. He pinches both my nipples at the same time, harder than I'm used to. My eyelids flare wide and energy zips back through my body at the slight pain.

"Get out of Vegas, Sondra Simonson."

That was the last thing I expected him to say after bringing me to orgasm with his clever mouth and fingers. Before he's gotten off.

He continues to make love to my breasts, squeezing them, thumbing my nipples. He lunges over me to flick his tongue over one stiff bud. "You're too bright a light for a seedy place like this. It will tarnish you." Another flick of his tongue. "*I* will tarnish you."

His words aren't jiving with his actions, so my brain is slow to catch up. What is he telling me?

"You came here for a fresh start. Your cousin's here. I get it. But you should've gone home to Marshall, Michigan, baby."

I shouldn't be surprised that he knows where I'm from, but hearing it sends a tingle up my spine. It's partly fear—or the awareness of how dangerous this man is. How thoroughly he researched me. But there's also an excitement in being the object of such intense scrutiny. Because clearly, he's into me.

He watches me intently as he tugs and rolls my nipples. There's conflict in his expression, or tension, and it grows exponentially every second. Suddenly, everything hardens. His jaw tightens, focus goes steely. "I'll give you money for a fresh start." He slaps my breast, and I cry out with surprise. "It's not payment for sex, so don't even go there." He points a warning finger at me. "I want you to take it and get out of town. Don't come back, *piccolina*."

I finally rouse myself past my orgasmic languor and push my back off the couch where I'm slumped. "What are you saying?" I frown at him. I can't figure out if he's threatening me or trying to help. I can't figure out what in the hell is going on here.

Nico moves in a flash, gripping under my armpits. Suddenly, I'm horizontal on the couch and he's looming over me. He slaps my breast again and I squirm beneath him, my hips bucking up to meet his. "I'm saying..." He rubs the back of his hand across his mouth. "I'm saying you should get out of here. I'm way too locked onto you, *bambina*. This is the last chance I'm gonna give you to

69

run." His eyes glitter dark and dangerous. "You set foot in this suite again, I'm going to claim you as mine. I'll chain you to my bed and fuck you every goddamn minute of the day."

I go still beneath him. My heart pounds against my ribs. I'd be lying if I said his words didn't thrill me. Oh, I hear the danger beneath them. The threat. But also, so much desire.

I've never been wanted this much by any man. I've always been the sort of pathetic, under-appreciated girl-friend. The one who catches her guy cheating with multiple women.

Knowing he wants me this much flushes me with heat. With power.

He gives a single nod. "You understand me." He eases off me and stands. With the gentleness of a parent dressing a small child, he slides my bra back over my breasts and zips my zipper.

He stands over me, as dark and forbidding as he'd been that first day. "I'm letting you go, Sondra Simonson." It's a pronouncement—like he's some kind of god, which, in his world, he is. I can imagine his employees falling to their knees when he speaks. "Run while you still can. Because once I decide you're mine, I will ruin you. Be sure of it." He stares at me a moment longer, his throat work-ing, then turns away.

His shoulders slump as he picks up my discarded panties from the floor and hands them to me.

My stomach knots and twists. The energy between us tangles, torques. There's so much in his words to dissect. He's letting me off the hook. Giving me an out. Or is he making me an offer? Or an ultimatum?

I can't figure it out, and I suddenly want to get the hell out of there. I yank on my panties without looking at him and stand up. I head toward the door, and he meets me at my cart and thrusts a neatly wrapped stack of hundred-dollar bills at me. "Take it," he says.

I jerk back like he slapped me.

"It's not a payment, it's a gift. Make a new start somewhere else. Not in my casino."

I ignore him and push my cart toward the door.

He catches my arm and turns me around. "Sondra. Take it." His chocolate brown eyes implore.

My nose burns and I shake my head. "I don't want your money." My throat is tight, although I have no reason to be upset. He gave me an orgasm and offered me money, which I really could use. Why, then, do I feel like I just got used and dumped?

"Please take it. It's nothing to me and it would give you options. I just want you to have options, Sondra. I don't want you to to make choices you'll regret."

I arch my brows. "Like what I just did with you?" I snap. "Well, it's too late for that."

I don't know why I'm pissed, but I am. I guess the offer of money does cheapen everything. Or maybe I'm mad he thinks he can make decisions about my life without consulting me. Either way, I've had it. I knew my infatuation with Nico Tacone was a mistake, and I need to crush it now before I get hurt even more.

"Sondra." His voice carries so much quiet command, I stop, my hand on the door handle.

"I'm sorry if I hurt or humiliated you. That wasn't my intent."

I don't know why I'm surprised to hear such emotional maturity out of a mob boss, but I am.

I shrug. "I'll get over it." I pull the door open and push my cart through.

"I'm not sorry for the rest of it," I hear him say just as I shut the door.

 *ico*

I'M itchy and ready to put my fist through the wall for the first thirty minutes after she leaves.

I hurt her. It was there, all over her face. I fucking tried to do the right thing, but she didn't see it that way.

And somehow hurting her is less conscionable than anything else. But the real question is—why was she hurt? Because I offered the money? Did I make her feel like a whore? I tried to be clear it wasn't because she let me into her panties. Or was it something else? Rejection?

Fuck, she doesn't deserve that.

And then the need to fix it takes over, way stronger than my desire to do the right thing for her. Or maybe I'm just a greedy bastard who's pretending he gives a fuck about anybody but himself.

I can't stay away from Sondra Simonson.

I pick up my phone and call security. "I need the location on an employee." All of our employee name tags have tracking devices and the information on where they are in the casino is easy to pull up. It's also recorded so we know where everyone's been in the case of an incident.

"Sure thing, Mr. Tacone, who are you looking for?"

"Name is Sondra Simonson. She works in house-keeping."

A pause. "I'm sorry, Mr. Tacone, it looks like she's off-premises."

Fuck. She quit.

I told her to. I shouldn't feel like flipping my desk over or heaving my chair through the glass door to my balcony.

She's smart. She heeded my warning.

Just to be sure, I hang up and call the manager of housekeeping. "I'm looking for one of your employees—Sondra Simonson. Is she working today?"

"I'm sorry, Mr. Tacone, she said she wasn't feeling well. I let her go home early. I sent Jenny up to clean the penthouse suites. Sondra told me she finished with yours—was that not true? Is there something else you need?"

She didn't quit. She went home sick.

"No, everything's fine." I end the call and stare at my phone. The idea of Sondra being upset enough to leave has me ready to fly out the door to chase her down. But I'm also relieved she didn't quit.

What does it mean?

Is she thinking about coming back here? After I made it plain what would happen? Fuck.

I really don't want to dim her light. But I should assuage any hurt feelings.

I call down to the casino florist. "I need three dozen roses delivered off-site right away."

"Of course, Mr. Tacone. Where are they going?"

I grab Sondra's file and read off her address.

"Color?"

"You pick."

"Note on the card?"

I hesitate. What in the hell do I say? I blow out my breath. "How about... *Can I take you to dinner tonight?* And sign it, *Nico.*"

"Perfect, Mr. Tacone, I'll send them out straight away."

"Thank you."

I hang up.

What am I doing? Now I want to take her to dinner? After I just tried to set her free? Fuck. I'm so fucked in the head over this woman, it's embarrassing.

I have a full-on infatuation with a woman I will likely destroy.

∼

Sondra

I TAKE THE BUS HOME. I didn't stop to tell Corey I was leaving because I need to get my head on straight. I didn't want to answer her questions about what happened and what I'm going to do.

I should quit.

He made it plain I should quit.

He also made it plain how much he wants me. Not just a one and done, either.

He wants to keep me.

At least that's what I read into his threats.

And damn if that doesn't appeal to me on some level. I've never had a man be so into me. I've been the girl who was easy to walk away from. Easy to cheat on.

And so part of me thinks I should defy him and just show up tomorrow. Dare him to make good on his threat.

But the rest of me can't take another emotional roller coaster. The possession and then rejection.

I get off at my stop and walk the six blocks to Corey's townhouse.

And...fuck. Dean's car is there. I was really hoping to have the place to myself. I literally have not been alone since I moved to Vegas. Not unless you count when I'm cleaning rooms.

And if I ever needed some alone time, it's now.

I almost keep walking. But it's hot out. And I want a shower. I need to wash Tacone off of me. Wash this day off me.

I walk in and find Dean on the couch watching television. His face lights up with a lazy grin. "Hey, Sondra."

Okay, yeah. He sounds a little too happy to see me.

"Hey," I mumble and grab a change of clothes from my suitcase beside the sofa. I walk past him to the bathroom.

He gets up and follows me. "I didn't think you'd be home today."

I ignore him and shut the bathroom door. Prick. I turn on the shower and let the water run. Maybe I'm being bitchy, but it's getting harder and harder to even be polite to Dean. I don't like the guy and he's giving me the creeps.

I take off my clothes and get in the shower, but any satisfaction I was hoping to derive from the water therapy is completed cancelled out by the knowledge that Dean is just beyond the door.

If there had been a peephole, he'd probably look through it.

Gross.

I end up cutting the shower short and hustling to get dressed. Maybe I will take that walk. It's like I can sense the omnipresent Dean energy seeping through the door. I seriously need some space.

When I walk out, I'm greeted by the sight of not one bouquet of roses, but three.

And one very sour looking Dean.

"Are these from your boss?" he demands. The asshole has opened the card. He tosses it to me. It flutters to the floor at my feet.

I stoop to pick it up and read it.

Nico Tacone is asking me to dinner? After he just ejected me from his suite?

This day couldn't get weirder.

"What did you do to make him send you roses?" Dean asks. When he takes a step closer, it feels menacing.

I don't like the insinuation. "Nothing."

Dean's scoff is derisive. "Yeah, right. Did you have sex with him?" He grabs my arm. "You should be careful. Did you know he's mafia?"

I twist to get out of his grip, but he closes his fingers tighter. "Ouch," I protest. "Get off me."

He steps even closer, leaning down so we're nose to nose. "I think you're real hot, Sondra," he says. His breath smells like Doritos. "I'm sure Tacone does too."

Again I try to pull away, but Dean holds me fast.

"Let go of me," I snap.

"I love that you and Corey are cousins," he says, backing me up against the wall. "It's almost as good as doing twins."

"You're not going to do me, so get that idea out of your head." My indignation is turning to panic now. I thought Dean was sleazy, but I didn't think he was the kind of guy to force a girl. But clearly I got it wrong. Because any normal guy would've let me go when I asked him to.

His fingers squeeze with bruising strength around my arm. He reaches his other hand between my legs.

"Get. The fuck. Off me." I'm genuinely struggling now, twisting to try to get out of his grasp, trying unsuccessfully to knee him in the nuts. He slams me against the wall.

A loud knock sounds on the door, and it provides just enough distraction for me to duck and wrench my arm out of his grasp. I run for the door like whoever is standing on the other side is my salvation.

"Sondra."

I ignore Dean's hiss and throw open the door, planning to run out under the protection of whoever is standing there.

I had no idea that person would be Nico Tacone.

I bump into him in my haste to step out and he catches me, brows dropping. He looks past me into the townhouse and his frown deepens.

"What's going on? Are you upset?" He steps back to survey me and doesn't miss the angry red marks on my arms.

That's all it takes. I didn't even say a word, but he goes marching into the townhouse and clocks Dean.

There's a sickening crunch of bone as his nose breaks and he goes flying back, stumbling against the couch and slipping to the ground. Tacone follows him and picks him up by his shirt to deck him again.

"Okay!" I yell. "Stop." I grab Tacone's arm.

He pauses to look at me. He's in his full designer suit, but he hasn't broken a sweat. "Sondra, go wait in the car." His voice is perfectly even, like meting out violent justice is all in a day's work for him. Which it probably is.

Oh Jesus. He's going to kill Dean.

I may be pissed off at what Dean did to me, but I already feel like we're even. I mean, the guy has blood gushing from his nose and he's on his ass.

"No." I attempt to tug Tacone toward the door. "Let's get that dinner. That sounded nice."

He drops Dean to the floor and straightens to face me. "Who is this guy? Did he hurt you?"

I wince because I know the answer is going to cause more violence. "He's my cousin's boyfriend. Please—can we go?"

Tacone reaches in his jacket. I know what he's going to pull out before he produces the gun because I've had the thing pointed at my head. He leans over and presses the barrel against Dean's temple. "Get out of here."

As terrified as Dean appears, he still sputters, "This is my place."

Tacone pistol whips him. "I said, get out of here. Get your shit. Move out. If you ever come near Sondra or her cousin again, I'll fucking kill you. Do you understand me?"

Dean doesn't answer fast enough and Tacone pulls the gun back to pistol whip him again. "Okay! I'm leaving!" He puts his hands in the air and slowly crawls to his feet.

Tacone doesn't take his eyes off Dean, but he murmurs to me, "Is that your bag, baby?"

It takes me a second to understand, but then I realize he's talking about my open suitcase beside the couch.

"Yeah. Yes, it is."

Tacone puts the gun back in the holster under his arm and strides over to the suitcase, closing it with a decisive zip.

I'm trembling like a leaf, possibly going into as much shock as I experienced the first time I saw Tacone's gun.

"Get in the car, baby." He grabs my suitcase by the handle and lifts his chin toward the door.

My knees wobble as I walk, but I manage to pick up my purse and toddle to the door. Tacone's right behind me, carrying my suitcase. Neither of us look back as we go out.

~

Nico

I HAD some romantic notion about treating Sondra like a lady and taking her on a date. That idea died a quick death when I saw the flare of fear in her eyes and the marks on her arms.

Fucking bastard. I seriously want to kill the mother-fucker for handling my girl.

Yeah, I may have been trying to pretend I hadn't already claimed Sondra Simonson, but I have.

It's too late for her.

The devil takes what the devil wants. And I want her.

I have the power of dark fury still running through my veins, which makes me feel invincible, but I try to rein it back.

Sondra's terrified. As scared as she was the day I met her. Fuck. Was it because of me? What I did back there? I have to remember she's not used to seeing guys get their noses broken.

I throw her suitcase in the trunk of the Lamborghini and open the passenger door for her. After I get in the driver side and start the car, I have to ask, "Sondra, he didn't—"

"No." She shakes her head. And then, to my utter demolishment, she bursts into tears.

"Baby." My hands grip the steering wheel tight enough to crush it. "Fuck."

"I'm okay." She sniffs. "It's just been a long day."

"I'm sorry. I know I'm part of that. Or maybe all of it?" I give her a sidelong glance.

She shakes her head.

Thank fuck.

"Y-you're not going to...do anything else to him. Right?"

Do I want to whack the guy? Totally. If she told me

he'd raped her, I definitely would. But no. The whole reason I left Chicago to open a casino in Vegas was because I wanted to get out of the underworld. I run a legit business. I keep the blood off my hands as much as possible.

"You want me to do anything else?" I just want to be sure.

She shakes her head quickly. No surprise there.

"Then, no. I won't touch him again. So long as he gets his ass out of there."

She twists her fingers in her lap. "What if he doesn't?"

I grind my teeth. "Then I'll make sure he does."

"Not by killing him."

I look over. Sondra Simonson put her foot down about something. I rather enjoy hearing the steel in her voice, almost as much as I like it when she yields to me. "Yeah, okay. I'll just relocate him."

She wipes at the drying tears on her face. "Where are you taking me?"

"To the Bellissimo. I'm going to get you a suite there— no charge, no obligation. You need a decent fucking bed to sleep in." I tinge my voice with finality and she doesn't argue. I can't stand knowing she's been sleeping in the townhouse with that asshole hovering nearby.

After a long moment, she gives a soft, "Thanks."

The squeeze of my heart surprises me. "For what?"

She picks at a thread on her jean shorts. "I'm glad you showed up when you did."

Now I want to go back and kill the guy. Not touching her is definitely no longer an option. I reach over and palm her nape, stroking my thumb along the column of her neck. "You tell me if you see that guy again."

It's the wrong thing to say. Sondra pales again and I feel a little shudder run through her.

Hell. She's scared of me. But maybe that's for the best. She should be scared of me. She should lock her door and stay way the fuck away.

~

Sondra

I'M SHAKY AND SHOCKED. Maybe that's why I'm not at all afraid of Nico Tacone this time. I'm actually feeling strangely comforted and cared for, which is stupid, because I know this man is incredibly dangerous. Heck, I just saw him pull a gun on someone. Again.

And yet, he was defending me, so suddenly his danger shifted into heroism. I know Corey would say I'm listening to *The Voice of Wrong* again.

And oh God! What will Corey say about Dean?

Will she blame me for this? Blame Nico when Dean leaves? Will Dean leave? I hope, for his sake, he does. Actually, I hope for all of our sakes.

Tacone pulls up to the front circle of the Bellissimo and steps out of the car. The valet rushes over to open my door. Tacone tosses him the keys. "There's a suitcase in the trunk."

"Of course, Mr. Tacone."

He escorts me inside, bypassing the line to reception

and walking straight up to an empty station. The bellhop trails us with my suitcase. One of the employees rushes over.

"I need a comp suite for Ms. Simonson."

Tacone's employees are well-trained because there's not a trace of curiosity in the receptionist's expression, only an efficient, eager-to-please attitude as her fingers fly over the keys. She looks at me and smiles. "How long will you be staying, Ms. Simonson?"

"Um...one or two—"

"Indefinitely," Tacone cuts in. "Close it off for the next few months at least."

Months? I was going to say nights. A suite at the Bellissimo runs $450 a night high season.

"Okay, I just need a picture ID and credit card for incidentals," the receptionist says, gaze sliding to Tacone.

I reach for my purse, but he gives an impatient shake of his head. "No charge for incidentals."

The buzzing that started in my chest when he said I could stay here for months gets louder. Nico Tacone is going to let one of his housemaids stay in a luxury suite and order room service to her heart's content for free? I know he likes me, but the warning bells are going off.

Tacone seems to notice, because he shoots me a look. It's one part warning, one part reassurance. *Just take it,* he seems to be saying.

"Okay, you're room 853, that's in the north tower. Take the elevator to your left." When the receptionist slides the card to me, Tacone takes it and hands it to the bellhop, dismissing him with a jerk of his chin.

The bellhop rolls soundlessly away with my bag.

Tacone places a hand at my lower back and guides me toward the bank of elevators. People glance at us as we go by. He's dressed in his beautiful suit and I'm in cut off jean shorts and a halter top. Crap, do I look like his whore?

My steps falter.

Tacone stops and turns me to face him. A muscle in his jaw tightens. "Take the fucking room," he snaps, like he already knows I was about to bail. He releases me and holds his hands up, fingers spread wide in surrender. "I'm not gonna go up with you. You don't have to see me again. You don't work for me. In fact, you're fired. And now you have a place to stay while you figure your shit out." He jerks his chin toward the elevator, where the bellhop is holding the door open for me. "Go."

He turns and walks away, not waiting to see what I'll choose. I hesitate. The bellhop has my suitcase, so I have to go get it, regardless.

I might as well find out what it's like to sleep in a Bellissimo suite.

Just for one night.

Tomorrow I can figure my shit out.

CHAPTER 6

BECAUSE I'M way too obsessed, the next day I check to see if Sondra quit or checked out. She didn't, but she did call in sick.

I search the casino video feeds until I eventually spot her lying out by the pool.

I smile. Good for her.

But then I wish I hadn't found her, because the urge to go out on the pool deck and rip that string bikini off her body and lick every place the sun hasn't touched overwhelms me. And that's closely followed by a blast of white hot jealousy. Because every fucking guy on the pool deck is seeing the same thing I am.

And something about a scantily clad Sondra Simonson is way more risqué than the showgirls and cocktail waitresses who parade around my club with more of their asses and tits showing.

I do the only thing reasonable—get the hell away from the security feeds and out on the floor, terrorizing my employees.

I see Corey on the floor and her eyes meet mine, bold and confrontational.

Yes, I handed your boyfriend his ass and told him to get out of your life. I may have a bit of a god complex. Sue me.

Because I'm feeling like a tyrant, I head right over to the floor manager, Ross. "Stand in for Corey Simonson for a moment. I need to have a word with her."

"Yes, sir, Mr. Tacone." Ross hustles over to Corey, who's working the roulette wheel, and murmurs something in her ear. As soon as the play is over, he steps in for her, making all her customers groan. People get superstitious about their croupier, especially when she's a tall, gorgeous redhead.

Corey lifts her chin and strides over to me, wearing the hell out of a pair of pumps and a slinky black dress with a plunging neckline.

"You have something to say to me?" I demand as soon as she arrives.

Her eyelids flare for a moment before she hides her surprise. She's silent a full beat. "No, sir."

"You sure?" I challenge.

Another beat, then she shakes her head. "I don't give a shit what you to do him." Disgust infuses her voice and I experience a flash of sympathy for her. It's a wonder how beautiful women end up with losers for boyfriends.

Cazzo, now I'm getting soft for other people, too. What in the hell is wrong with me? I definitely need some fucking sleep.

~

Jenna

"I⊤'s time to seal the deal," my father pronounces. He's sitting behind his great walnut desk, snipping the end off a cigar. I've been summoned here, to his office, the mafia princess to the king.

The knot of anxiety I've carried under my ribs from the time I was old enough to understand my future cinches up so tight I can't breathe.

"Junior Tacone asked about you. He knows you graduated college. I can't put it off any longer."

I curse the tears that spring into my eyes. But it isn't fair. I've been trapped into this marriage since I was nine months old. Signed over to marry a man ten years older than I am. A man who never wanted me, either.

I guess that should be my one comfort.

"Did Nico ask for me?" My voice wobbles.

My father lights the cigar and puffs.

I hate cigar smoke. I can't stand the way my dad blows it in my direction like he's never heard of second-hand smoke health issues.

"No. I don't know what the fuck Nico's problem is. If he thinks he's going to disrespect this family by refusing to marry you—"

"But I don't want to marry him," I wail, for the four hundred and fiftieth time.

My dad points an imposing finger at me. "You'll do what you have to do to solidify the bond between our families. That's the one fucking thing I ask of you. You don't have to get your hands dirty, don't have to be a soldier like your brothers. You marry who I fucking tell you to marry, and you do it with class. The way your mother raised you."

And this is the answer I've heard my entire life.

I swallow back the bile rising in my throat.

"The families have been bonded all these years just with the marriage contract. We don't need an actual wedding to solidify things."

"Enough." My father waves a hand. "I'm sending you to Vegas. You tell Nico Tacone to start making wedding plans. The time has come."

∼

Sondra

AFTER THREE DAYS of a luxury vacation on Nico Tacone's dime, I decide it's time to go back to work. And I'm fully aware what that means.

He warned me, thoroughly.

He's also honored his word and stayed away. No contact, unless you count his talking to Corey. But I haven't had any leads on a professional job and this one is better than nothing.

Oh, who am I kidding? Going back to work means I've decided to offer myself up like a virginal sacrifice to Nico Tacone.

He's like an addiction. I want to stay away—I really do. I know it's the right thing. But the excitement produced by the thought of seeing him again is too hard to resist. I want to be near him again, to sizzle and sear under the flame of his desire for me.

Quit the job. Move back to Michigan. Use your degree, the voice of reason argues.

Mine, says *The Voice of Wrong,* pawing the air in the direction of Nico's suite with cat claws.

So I show up to work and pack my housekeeping cart like nothing happened.

"Feeling better?" Marissa asks.

"Yep. It was a stomach bug." I feel a little guilty about lying to her, but what can I do? The real story is too bizarre to share with anyone but Corey.

I'm hoping she bounces back from the Dean thing soon. She came over to the suite the night it happened and the two of us drank a couple bottles of wine until we were cursing all men and vowing to never let each other date a loser again.

Which, of course, meant Corey tried to talk me out of my infatuation with Tacone. So now I'll have her judgment to face on top of whatever trouble I get myself into today. But she'll be there to pick up the pieces for me.

Maybe that's the lesson in all this. I pick shitty men, but there are people in my life who love me and would do anything for me. That's a gift all on its own.

I clean the other suites first. In the second one, I run into the guys I saw on the first day.

"That's the one," one of them mutters to the other as they leave and I go in.

"What one?"

"The housekeeper Nico's obsessed with." The door clicks shut. It's not really new news. I know he has a thing for me. But hearing it from a stranger's lips makes it more solid. More real. More exciting. I have a bounce in my step as I clean.

When I'm finished, I head into Tacone's suite. He's not there, which is definitely for the best. It's a stay of execution. So why, then, am I so disappointed?

I'm almost finished with the last room when I hear Tacone's keycard in the lock.

My heart shoots into my throat.

Tacone saunters in and his gaze takes in the housekeeping cart, then swivels around to see me. The moment our eyes connect, a jolt of pure electricity zaps me where I stand.

There's satisfaction in Tacone's small smirk, and dark promise in his eyes.

He stalks toward me. "I did warn you what would happen if you came back, right?" His voice is rough, hungry.

I hold his gaze. "You warned me."

He reaches me, shaking his head. "You asked for it." He picks me up by the waist and plops me on the barstool that cozies up to the breakfast bar. I reach for his belt, but he grabs my wrist.

"Nuh uh. I'm in charge, baby. I decide when and how

I'm gonna fuck you. Whether I'm going to satisfy my fantasy of bending you over that housekeeping cart, or make you put those pigtails back in your hair and take you in the shower." He slides his palms up my bare legs, pushing the skirt of my housekeeping dress up as he goes. When his thumbs reach my panties, he slides them lightly over the gusset, teasing me.

My pussy squeezes around air. I grab his arms to keep from falling back.

"That's right, sugar. You hang on tight. Because this time I'm not holding back."

The sound that comes out of my throat is unrecognizable.

He brushes his knuckle over my clit, barely making contact, driving me crazy. "Did you bring this pussy to me to get fucked? You knew I wouldn't let her go empty this time, didn't you?"

It's dirty and crude, but God help me, I love it. Lord, if Tanner had ever talked to me this way, I would've laughed in his face. But Tacone pulls it off because he oozes sexual confidence.

My head wobbles as I nod.

That's what brought me back here. I want another Nico Tacone orgasm. I just have to remember to keep my head about me and not let my heart get involved. And to avoid witnessing anything illegal that could put me in danger.

Yeah, I'm stupid. I'm a horny little idiot who's certain this is going to be the best lay of my life.

He tucks a thumb under the gusset of my panties. "Mmm hmm. You're wet for me, aren't you?" I guess I'm readier than I've ever been, because he slips his thumb right in me without any preparation needed. He groans, his lids drooping. "*Bambina*...I've been thinking about this pussy every minute of the day since the day I first caught you here." He holds me around my waist, tipping me back and pumps his thumb. "Whole casino full of pussy, but I only want this one."

My head falls back. I'm balanced on my tailbone, arched over his arm, my upper body kept up by my grip on his forearms.

"And this is why. You're so fucking *inviting*. So *receptive*." His face contorts as if it pains him not to be inside me.

I squirm, wanting to take him deeper, get more friction. His thumb is not enough.

"Greedy girl. You want me to fuck you good?"

"Yes, please."

He gives a pained bark of laughter. "And you fucking say *please*. Every time. Sweetest girl I've ever had." He withdraws his thumb and pulls me off the barstool. "Turn around, *bambi*."

I whirl and put my forearms on the barstool, pushing my ass out. He yanks my panties down and then off before he slaps my ass.

I never thought I'd be into pain, but after that spanking he gave me last time, I'm not just ready for it, I crave it. He slaps my ass again, and again. Each time is a shock of pain, a splash of pleasure. I'm drowning in sensation, falling deeper and deeper into an abyss of lust and desire.

"Please," I whimper.

He gives a sharp curse. "Push your ass out, beautiful."

My ass is already out, but I try to arch even more. I hear the snap of a condom wrapper and I wait as he rolls on protection. He rubs the head of his cock along my slit.

I push back at him, trying to get him inside me. I can't stand another second of this teasing. I need satisfaction.

He pushes into me with a hard thrust and the barstool tips and rights again. "Fuck." He pulls out and I nearly weep. I must've whimpered, because he soothes me. "It's okay, *bambi*. Lay over the arm of the sofa here. I need to fuck you way harder than I can here."

I toddle to the sofa and he pushes me over the arm and slaps my ass again.

"You look so goddamn perfect with my handprints on your ass, Sondra Simonson."

I don't know why he always says my first and last name, but I love it. It makes me feel like someone famous. A movie star or a superhero. As promised, he plows into me so deep I cry out.

He stays there, cupping my throat to lift my head. "Okay?"

He's checking in with me. He may talk a tough game, but Nico is considerate. When he's not pointing a gun at someone's head.

I arch back. "Yeah."

He doesn't move. "Yeah, what?"

My mind stutters, not sure what he wants. "Yes, sir?"

He chuckles. "Baby, you keep calling me *sir* and you're going to get fucked until tomorrow. Ask me for what you want. I want to hear you say please again in that sweet little voice that makes my balls so tight."

"Please, Nico."

"Fuck."

He withdraws and slams into me, taking my breath away with the force of it. It's too rough, too hard, but I wouldn't complain if it killed me. It feels so right. So good. He fucks me hard, his loins slapping against my ass like a second spanking, his cock drilling deep inside my sopping channel.

"Please." Now that I know what he wants, what makes him crazy, I'm going to keep saying it.

He curses again and grips my upper arms, arching my upper back as he pounds into me.

I whimper but I spread my legs wider, work to relax my muscles to better receive the full force of his thrusts. My mind is lost. I haven't even come yet, but I'm rocketing into outer space. No, somewhere better than outer space. The place of no thought. Only pleasure. Only ripe, juicy, satisfying, pounding pleasure.

"Yes, Nico, *please*," I whine.

"Stop begging, baby." His voice is rough. "Stop begging or I won't last another—fuuuuuuuck." He buries himself deep and bucks his hips against my ass, coming.

Somehow, he still has the wherewithal to remember I haven't come and he lifts my hips away from the sofa enough to get his hand under me and rub my clit.

I go off, fireworks splintering in front of my eyes, my body convulsing under his rough touch.

I'm stuffed full of his cock, dancing against his fingers for long moments—for an eternity. And then it's over and I forget how to breathe.

I collapse over the arm of the sofa, my vision black.

No, my eyes are closed. I don't know how long I've been lying limp like that, but Nico eases out and it rouses me.

"Come here, baby. Let's get you cleaned up." He spins me around. I can hardly stand on my two feet. I definitely can't focus.

His smile is indulgent right before he bends at the waist and places his shoulder against my hip. And then I'm in the air, tossed over his shoulder, my bare ass to the sky. He gives it a slap as he carries me to his bathroom. He holds me like a sack of potatoes as he turns on the water to the shower, then puts me down and pulls off my dress.

"I wanted to fuck you in here, little girl. That first day I found you cleaning. I put you in the shower and it was all I could do not to strip and follow you in." He strips now and I stand there, still a rag doll. "It was totally depraved. And then I heard you crying, and I felt like an even bigger asshole."

I don't know what to say, because it is depraved that he wanted to fuck me after what he'd done. And yet, hearing it only brings me the thrill of power I get every time he talks about how much he desires me.

This incredibly wealthy, powerful, dangerous man thinks I'm his weakness.

It makes me giddy with power.

And stupid. Because this is just about sex. It's an infatuation, for whatever reason. And I'd better watch out or I could find myself in real danger.

"You're not really going to keep me prisoner here." I say it like a statement, but it's really a question. I have to ask, now that my brain is returning and the adrenaline of fear is starting to return.

His lids droop to half-mast. He pushes me into the spray of water and follows me in. I find myself pinned against the beautiful Italian marble wall and his hands coast over my breasts, down my sides.

"Am I going to let you go? It's debatable. Not until I fuck you at least one more time."

My anxieties fade. He's not insane. He wouldn't really tie me to the bed—not if I didn't want it. Not the guy who stopped to make sure I was okay when I whimpered during sex.

I didn't think so, but I needed to be sure.

He grabs a bar of soap and lathers it in both hands, then strokes the suds across my shoulders, then over my breasts. He soaps my belly, down my outer thighs, then he turns me around and gets my back, my ass.

He starts to stroke between the crack of my ass.

My legs, already unsteady, start shaking. It's both embarrassing and arousing to have my anus so thoroughly cleaned, massaged and stroked.

"I bet this juicy ass has never been fucked before."

I stiffen, because, yeah. I'm totally an anal virgin and I'm definitely not into giving it up to him.

He reaches around the front of me and cups my mons, stroking the tender flesh there ever so lightly. "You're afraid." He brings his lips to my ear and then nips me there. "That shouldn't excite me."

My knees lock and I swerve my hips away from him. I definitely don't want this. Especially not when it sounds like he wants to force it on me.

He turns me around and cages my throat with his hand. He doesn't squeeze, just uses it to hold me still for a harsh kiss. Water runs down my face, between our lips. He moves his mouth over mine, fucking me with his tongue, twisting and turning his lips over mine, changing the angle, devouring me.

After a moment I relax into him, open for the onslaught.

His hands coast around to my ass and he squeezes, cupping and kneading my cheeks as he makes love to my face.

His cock hardens against my belly. "I need you again, *bambi*. Are you going to give it to me like a good girl?"

Those words shouldn't turn me on, but they do. My pussy clenches, pelvic floor lifts. I wrap one leg around his waist and invite him in.

He groans against my lips. "I forgot to bring a condom in." He removes my leg from his waist and pushes me against the shower wall. "Move from this position and I'll spank your ass pink. *Capiche*?"

"Yeah." I'm breathless.

He leans in and kisses me again, hard and twisty lipped. "So sweet." But then he points a warning finger at me as he backs out of the shower. It's a gesture that makes my knees weak. It probably makes his enemies piss themselves, his underlings jump into line.

He's back a moment later, already rolling the condom on. He crowds against me, leaning his forehead against mine, his cock sawing between my legs.

"You too sore for this?"

There it is again—the consideration. I don't know why it always surprises me. I guess because the rest of the time he can be so harsh. It's so damn appealing, this mixture of asshole and tenderness. It makes him beyond attractive.

I am too sore, but I can't refuse more sex. Not because I don't want to disappoint him. Because I need it. Even with the orgasms he already gave me, I'm hungry for more. Want to know how this scene ends.

"Not too sore." My voice sounds scratchy.

He presses his thumb in my mouth and I suck on it. "I don't do gentle, *amore*. You'd better know that."

He pulls his thumb out enough for me to answer, "Are you warning me off again?"

He kicks my feet wider, then lifts my thigh, but instead of putting it on his hip where it was before, he slaps my pussy.

I gasp. My nipples harden to diamond points.

He spanks between my legs again. It's a punishment of some sort, but I'm not sure what it's for. Or maybe he just likes to hurt me.

It wouldn't surprise me if the mafia kingpin was a sadist. His world is crime and violence.

But then he melds his mouth over mine and lines up his cock with my entrance. "Take it, then." His voice is gruff and deep. He thrusts in, filling me.

I throw my arms around his shoulders and claw the back of his neck. He shoves up, lifting my other foot from the shower floor. I wrap it around his waist and he cups my ass. "You gonna ride my cock good, *bambina*?"

My pussy clenches, even as I'm offended. Is this the way he talks to the whores he usually uses?

But then I forget my ire in the next moment because he starts muttering against my neck as he plows in and out, "So sweet. So fucking good. This pussy could save a man, I swear to *Madonna*."

My upper back presses against the shower wall and he guides my movements, lifting and lowering me as he angles his thrusts up into me.

The heat of the water and steam, combined with the frantic sex makes me lightheaded.

Nico's rough, no doubt about it. I have no control over our movements—he's driving and he knows exactly what he wants and what he's doing. My moans take on a higher and higher pitch and then I'm squeezing around his cock, slapping his shoulder.

"Don't come," he commands. "Don't fucking come until I tell you to."

Again, I'm offended. I can't tell if it's supposed to be hot or he's just that controlling. Except it is hot. So hot, I can't help but obey him, just because I need to know what the reward for obedience will be.

Just because I'm desperate to reap my reward.

Nico's panting, shoving harder and faster, flattening me against the cool tile, the stubble of his five-o'clock shadow scraping and scratching my neck.

He shifts one of the hands on my ass to brush my crack and I jerk as a jolt of sensation sizzles through me.

My heart beats too fast, too hard. I'm too hot—I fear I'll pass out from the steam and the sex. He keeps brushing the tip of his finger over my anus, and the sensation ignites me.

A low growl echoes off the shower walls and his movements grow jerky. He mutters a string of filthy curses—half in English, half in Italian. Then he roars and shoves deep, biting my neck as he comes.

At the same time, the bastard breaches my anus with the tip of his finger.

I want to hate it, but it's too good. The sensation in my ass is awful and incredible. I go off like a shotgun, coming around his thick cock as his finger eases in a gentle pumping motion.

I choke on a strangled cry, my inner thighs squeezing hard enough to break his hips as my spasming channel milks his cock for any last fluid remaining.

And when it stops, I'm wrecked. A low sob comes from my throat. Tears sting my eyes, but it's only from the release. From the incredible, life-changing, orgasmic release.

Tacone croons something in Italian and turns off the water. He carries me out of the luxury shower and drapes a towel around my wet back.

I hardly register what's happening. My body's gone limp and my mind hasn't returned from my trip to outer space.

Nico lays me on my back on his giant bed and wraps the ends of the towel around my front. Then he flops down beside me. Before my brain clears of the fog stirring, his snores cut through the room.

I guess good sex is always the cure for insomnia.

Smiling, I ease away from him and off the bed, then find my clothes in the living room and get dressed.

I didn't finish dusting, but I skip it. I'm pretty sure he won't report me.

Actually, maybe he'll punish me for it.

And that thought has me smiling even wider.

I push my housekeeping cart out. Tony, his beefy bodyguard, is coming off the elevator headed toward Nico's room. "Is Mr. Tacone in there?" he asks.

"Yes, but he's sleeping."

Tony halts in his tracks, then turns back to face me with interest burning in his expression. He takes in my wet hair, my flushing cheeks. I ignore him, hitting the elevator button several more times.

Tony leans his back against Nico's door. "You have something to do with him sleeping?"

I shrug, but can't stop the smile playing around my lips. "Maybe."

Tony shakes his head. I'm thinking he's going to say something offensive, but instead he breathes, "Thank fuck."

The elevator dings and the doors slide open. I escape inside with my cart, eager to call Corey and tell her everything.

CHAPTER 7

THERE'S an actual spring in my step as I stride through my casino the next day. I slept sixteen hours and woke up with a boner hard enough to pound a nail. I didn't let myself rub one out, either, because now that I've finally dipped my cock in Sondra's tight little pussy, nothing else will do.

I knew it would be that way.

She'd better not run, because I'm not about to let her out of my clutches now.

First thing I did when I woke was make sure she hadn't checked out of the suite I put her in. She hadn't. And her employee name tag was sitting in the room, so chances were good she was there, still sleeping.

Everything seems to be in perfect order at the casino. Things went on without me. I stop at the business office to verify the income from the night before, and start to respond to the forty-seven texts I received while I slept like a bear in hibernation.

Meanwhile, I'm famished.

And somehow, I end up on the eighth floor, standing outside the suite where I put Sondra. I pull my keycard out.

I'm a first class asshole for not knocking. I'm definitely not acting like the gentleman my mamma raised me to be. But I can't deny the pleasure it gives me—the sheer sense of power and ownership, to slip my keycard into the lock and open the door.

Sorry, bambina. *I warned you I was trouble.*

It's another fucking wet dream, because I find Sondra in her panties and bra, standing at the mirror in the bathroom. Her head snaps up in surprise, but I don't give her a chance to say anything, because I'm stalking toward her like a starving man headed for his next meal.

She's an angel, her full lips parting in surprise, blue eyes wide but not frightened.

No, they're trusting.

And that should bring my sense back enough to have some decency. To treat her with some respect and courtesy.

But instead it only fuels my power-crazed lust for her.

She's going to let me.

Again.

It's written all over her face.

I move right in for the kill. Wrap my fist in the back of her soft hair and tug her head back for a kiss at the same time I meld my body to hers.

She opens for it. Her lips move against mine, and I swear to Christ, she pushes her pelvis out to meet me.

"Baby. You're too beautiful." I mouth fuck her harder, with more insistence. I back her against the bathroom counter and lift her soft ass up on it. "You gonna part those legs for me again, sweetheart? I'm already addicted to your pussy."

She opens her knees, arches her breasts up to me.

I growl and push the cups of her bra down to play with her nipples. "I slept all fucking night. From the time you left until 6 o'clock this morning."

She probably has no idea what I'm talking about—how would she know I haven't slept in months?

But she smiles—like she's genuinely happy to hear it. "I know." She actually looks smug. It's so adorable I try to kiss the lips right off her face.

I bring the pad of my thumb between her legs and stroke the tiny swatch of satin separating me from heaven. "How's your sweet little pussy today? Still sore?"

She sucks her lower lip between her teeth, which makes my thickened cock go rigid. "Yeah."

"You gonna let me in there again, anyway?"

She doesn't answer, so I lean down and flick my tongue over her nipple. "Need some convincing first?"

She weaves her fingers into my hair. "Yeah."

Challenge accepted. I still can't get the sound of her sweet little *yes, pleases* out of my head from yesterday. I can't wait to make her beg me for satisfaction again.

I continue a light, slow stroking over her panties while I suck and pinch her right nipple. It's pebbled up—has been since I walked in. "Bambi, you have the best set of tits in Nevada. Probably the only real set, too."

"Corey's are real."

"Corey's aren't half as hot as these." I don't want my girl comparing herself to her cousin. Maybe she doesn't—I don't really know. But Corey has an exotic beauty that might make some girls envious. It doesn't do anything for me. Sondra is my new and only template for the perfect female. Smart, sexy, freakishly sweet. A little naughty. Way too nice.

The need to possess her overwhelms me. I want to flip her around and bang her hard from behind, but I dial it back. I have big plans that involve her begging and pleading my name.

I move to her left nipple. Her panties grow damp under my thumb. I slip it inside and tap her clit.

Her teeth snap shut and she throws her head back. "You like that?"

She rocks her pelvis forward.

"Hmm?"

"Uh huh."

"You need my tongue between those legs?"

"Um…" She's pulling my mouth back to her nipple.

"I think you do. Spread wider, Sondra. And pull your panties to the side so I can taste you."

Her knees snap open and she pulls the panties away.

I swear to Christ I never thought I'd find myself on my knees for any girl. Now twice in two days I've contorted my body to get at this magic pussy. I'd do fucking anything just to have another taste. I throw a folded towel on the floor and drop down, pulling her pussy right up against my mouth.

Two licks and she's moaning, tearing at my hair. Her pussy gets wet, wet, wet, and it's not just from my tongue. I tap her clit while I make my tongue stiff and penetrate her with it. Then I lick all along her slit, tracing the inner lips. When I finally suction my mouth over her clit, she screams.

"Please, Nico!" She clamps her thighs around my ears.

"That's it."

I can't wait any longer. I rise and pull her off the counter, spin her around to face the mirror. "Push that ass out for me, little girl."

She obeys.

I yank her panties down and off and nudge her feet wider. I can't get the condom on fast enough. "Pinch your nipples," I command as I roll it over my length.

I get to watch her face in the mirror when I enter her —the way her mouth softens and jaw drops open. The flutter of her lashes as her eyes roll heavenward. I fill her slowly, feeding inch after inch into her tight channel.

She whimpers and arches her back more.

"Does it hurt?"

"No." It still sounds like a whimper. "I just want it so badly."

Ah, fuck. She shouldn't have said that. Because now I can't hold back—not even for a second. I grip her hips and start fucking her like there's no tomorrow. I'm careful to protect the front of her pelvis from banging against the marble countertop, which means I gotta hold her hips away. It's not enough. I can't smack in hard enough, can't get deep enough.

I loop an arm around her waist so her hips will hit my arm instead of the counter and now I can fuck her as hard as I need to.

My vision goes blurry, my thighs are already shaking. I slam into her, lights exploding behind my eyes on every instroke.

I need her.

I need this.

So much.

I can't stop. Can't wait. I can't even—-

I roar, cum shooting down my shaft. I slam in deep and stay there, my lips against the back of her head.

It feels so fucking good, I forget completely about satisfying her.

Fortunately, she found it on her own, because her pussy starts squeezing my cock, the muscles contracting in short bursts of perfection.

I could die right then and be happy.

I'm a man who has every material thing, and not an ounce of pleasure in his life. Not a fucking drop of happiness.

But right now, in this moment, I'm buoyant. Flying, even.

I close my eyes and listen to my own heartbeat pounding against her back. It slows with her breath.

And then I'm grateful. I kiss her neck, her shoulder, her ear. I find her temple and press my lips there. "Thank you," I murmur. It's not like me to thank anybody. I'm not that guy.

I'm the asshole who takes what he wants.

And I just did.

But now I'm thanking her. I would do anything she asked of me at this point.

What the fuck is wrong with me?

"You want some food, baby?"

"I don't have time before work," she murmurs.

Something closes off in my solar plexus. I can't stand sending her off to work after what we just did. Especially not to work for me. Especially not cleaning. My girl shouldn't be cleaning rooms for a living. She's a fucking professor.

I may have had a minor fetish for her prancing around my suite in that tight little pink dress, but it feels dead wrong.

Still, I can't offer her money for sex, instead. I'm not going to make a whore out of her.

"You're not working today," I growl.

She stiffens, whether it's from my bossy tone or what I said, I can't be sure. Her hair falls over her face, curtaining it from my view. "I just called in sick three days in a row. I think I'd better show up." She lifts her head and meets my eyes in the mirror. "And you're not calling in for me. I don't want people knowing I'm sleeping with the boss."

My jaw tightens and I pull out to dispose of the condom. The fist in my solar plexus squeezes harder. Everything's wrong about this, but I can't quite figure out how to make it right. And I've even had a decent night's sleep. Fuck, this girl has me ass over heels for her.

I want to say *you're fired*. I really do. But I know she needs the money. And also, I'm a terrible, selfish bastard and the worst part of me wants to keep her here, under my thumb. Under my watch. I like her calling me her boss, as wrong as it is.

I button my pants and take my phone out of my pocket. I call Samuel, the head of housekeeping, while Sondra skirts around behind me and gets dressed.

"Listen, I need to talk to you about Sondra Simonson, the housekeeper who cleans the penthouse suites."

"Yes, Mr. Tacone."

How am I going to make this work in a way that doesn't piss Sondra off or embarrass her? It may not be possible. Samuel is going to have to know I'm fucking her.

I sit on the edge of her bed to watch her dressing. "I'm trying her out for a new position." I wince when Sondra whirls around and glares at me. "She won't have time to clean the other two penthouse suites. Only mine. I have some additional personal assistant and errand work for her to do when she's in my suite."

Sondra puts her hands on her hips. Her lips press into a thin line.

I put the phone on speaker so she can hear how calmly Samuel takes this. "Of course, Mr. Tacone. Starting today?"

"Yes. I've already spoken to her about it, but you can tell her to report directly to my suite when she begins."

"Any change in her hourly?"

"Yes, double it."

Samuel clears his throat. "Absolutely. I'll let HR know, unless you already have."

"I haven't. Tell them to make it effective today, but this new position is on a trial basis."

"Understood. How long is the probationary period?"

I flick my gaze back to Sondra. How long can I keep her? How long before she smartens up and leaves? Before she finds the kind of job she deserves? Before I stop ruining her life?

"Four weeks."

"Thank you, Mr. Tacone."

I hang up without thanking him back, because I'm that kind of asshole.

Sondra looks torn between being pissed off and crying. Tragically, it's a look I've put on her face before. Several times.

I hold my arms out. "Come here, please."

There. I even said *please*.

She probably would've come without it, but I'm trying to soothe her. She walks over to me, wariness flickering over her expression.

I pull her to stand between my legs and stroke the sides of her hips. "He doesn't think anything, baby. He knows I would fucking nail his dick to the wall if he even considered thinking something about my personal life."

Her lips tug up in a reluctant smile. "What's this personal assistant job?"

I slide my hands around to cup her ass. "I'm not gonna pay you to have sex with me, baby. Because that would be an insult, and I've already offended you that way before." I slide my hands down her thighs, then up inside the skirt. "I just couldn't have you in those other guys' rooms. I would have to fucking kill them for looking at you in that dress. And I'd spank your ass red for doing any form of service for another man. Even if it's your job. Understand?"

She shifts, squeezing her thighs together like I've just turned her on instead of spewed some irrational possessive bullshit that ought to make her run for the hills.

"Okay," she says. "Thanks, I guess."

I pick the phone back up and glance at the time. "So you go punch in, and I'll order room service. What do you want for breakfast?"

Her face splits into a brilliant smile that makes me want to get on my knees and lick her until she screams again. "Pancakes and bacon. And the berries and whipped cream. And a half of a grapefruit."

I squeeze her hip and stand to give her a quick kiss. I want to spoil this girl, and the fact that she's letting me this time produces a satisfaction almost as powerful as claiming her.

～

Sondra

HE CAN'T STAY AWAY from me. I shouldn't be so giddy about it, but I am. I know this roller coaster ride probably ends in disaster, but I just can't get off.

I head to the housekeeping office to punch in. Of course Nico's patronizing me by keeping me on as his personal housekeeper. If I had any pride or sense, I'd get my butt back to Corey's place and refuse to play his out his *fuck the housekeeper* fantasies.

Especially considering the looks I get from the other maids when I show up.

Fuck. All 6080 Bellissimo employees probably know I'm sleeping with the boss by now.

I punch in and push the housekeeping cart up to Tacone's penthouse suite. He's not there yet, and I get started fast, wanting to finish quickly in case he wants to hang out.

The room service arrives before he does. It's awkward answering the knock, but the waiter bows. "Good morning, Ms. Simonson. Where would you like the food?"

Oh holy hell. He's giving his staff my name. I point to the table by the wall of windows and he leaves it there.

Nico comes in a few minutes later. I'm back in the bedroom, making the bed. "What the fuck are you doing?" he demands.

I should be used to his gruff manner by now, but I'm not. Still, I toss my pigtails as I turn. "What do you mean?"

"I invited you to breakfast, not to clean my fucking room."

"I thought you got off on watching me clean."

His lips twitch. He holds out his hand and my feet move to obey the gesture before my mind has even considered if it's wise. I put my hand in his and he leads me to the living room and pulls a chair at the table out for me. "I definitely do, *bambina*. But I don't want you to feel like a whore." His tone is still curt. Impatient. He hasn't sat down at the table with me, either. I get the feeling he's not staying.

"So then I should actually do my job, right?"

He sighs. "No, fuck it. Let's be honest. I do want you to

be my whore. You'll put on that outfit and prance around this suite for me, and I'll pay any amount you ask of me—on the payroll or cash. So now you know. Think about your terms."

I stare at him, too stunned to speak.

"Listen, I have to go—shit's come up. I have family coming into town tonight, but can I take you to dinner tomorrow?"

I'm reeling. Good sense says get the hell out here. *The Voice of Wrong* says, "Sure."

"Good. I'll pick you up at six." He takes a strawberry from the berry dish and holds it to my lips.

It's hard to meet the intensity of his dark gaze as I take a bite.

Nico turns the bitten strawberry and looks down at it, then opens his mouth and finishes what's left.

A shiver runs down my spine. But that's stupid. It was just a strawberry. It's not like he just completed some mafia ritual that forever bound me to him.

CHAPTER 8

ico

I'M LIKE A JEDI KNIGHT. I swear I feel the ripple in the force field when my brother enters the state. I am no longer king of my hill.

The big dog is in town.

Junior is the first born, ten years older than I am, and scary as fuck. As a kid, there were times I was sure he would kill me. He'd hold my head under the water in the pool until I started to pass out, or sit on me and box my ears until I'd do anything and everything he asked me to. Our father didn't tell him to lay off, probably because he raised Junior and my other brothers the same way. Violence is part of our world. It was part of our family life, too.

I never took my shit out on my younger brother, though. I looked out for Stefano, protected him from our big brothers, cousins and father. And in return, he became forever loyal to me. We were three years apart, but tight. His faith in me is probably the reason I had the courage to try to do something different instead of following in my father's footsteps.

And I've been minimizing my success in the family's eyes ever since. Because the last thing I want is the rest of them moving in on my territory.

So Junior's arrival has me on edge.

I sent Tony in a limo to pick them up at the hangar and he texts me to say he's on his way to the casino. I head down to the front to greet them personally, because family gets the royal treatment.

My employees greet me with deference. The valet parking attendants and bellhops stop their chatter and stand erect like fucking British soldiers protecting the queen.

When the limo pulls up, I open the back door myself, helping my ma out of the vehicle. I get four cheek kisses, back and forth, and a whole lot of greeting with broad hand gestures.

Even being around the soldiers I took from Chicago—Tony, Leo and my cousin Sal—I'm stunned by how *Sicilian* my mom is. Vegas has rubbed off on me, softened the old world air that still hangs on Junior and my mother.

I get a back-thumping hug from Junior. Tony tosses the keys to the valet and makes sure the bellhop gets their bags from the trunk. I escort them up to their luxury suites, listening to my mom's chatter the entire way about the latest on every family member. I'm only half-listening

118

until she says, "The Pachino girl is out of college now, Nico."

Only long practice of hiding emotions from the narrowed gaze of my big brother keeps me from showing anything on my face. We're in the elevator, which makes it all the more oppressive. "Oh yeah? Good for her."

"You need to make contact with Giuseppe," Junior says. "I already have."

The muscles in my neck stiffen. Now is the time. I've been silent on this issue far too long. "Yeah, I will. I'm not marrying her."

My mother goes still and Junior rotates fully to face me. "The fuck you're not."

"You're not boss," I snarl.

Junior's expression turns cold and hard. I've seen him kill wearing that same deadened look.

I shove my hands in my pockets and lower my gaze, forcing myself to appear more congenial. "Listen, I'll talk to Pops about it. I think we can come to some other arrangement that's equally beneficial for the Tacones and the Pachinos."

There. I said it. And that's all I have in my defense. I don't have any other ideas because this is an issue I've purposely refused to think about for most of my life.

The elevator arrives on their floor and I escort them out.

Junior snorts. "You'd better do it soon, then. I talked to Pachino last week. He's waiting for completion."

I find it hard to believe Pachino is that anxious when no one has said a word to me about it since the girl turned eighteen. If they were in a rush, they would've pushed the issue four years ago.

I run my fingers through my hair.

Cazzo.

"I'll take care of it."

"You'd better." The flint in his voice is the kind that brings men to their knees.

I slide the keycard into the lock of my ma's room and open the door. "After you," I murmur and she starts up again on her breathless report about everything and everyone back home.

CHAPTER 9

ondra

"I CHANGED MY MIND," I tell Corey, my cell phone pinched between my ear and my shoulder as I pace around on the balcony of my Bellissimo suite. "I don't want to go on this date."

"Okay, so you don't have to," she says patiently. "You don't have to stay there. You don't have to work there. I'll come pick you up right now."

She stopped by after her shift earlier and I filled her in on the latest. Now I've called her at home to talk some more.

I peer over the edge of the balcony at the busy strip below. "A quick crazy fling with Nico Tacone is one thing, but dating him? It's a bad idea."

"Agreed," Corey says. "So cancel the date."

"I don't even have his phone number. I have to wait until he shows up."

"What are you really worried about? Just say it, even if you think it sounds stupid."

Corey knows me so well.

"I have nothing to wear," I blurt. That's not really what this is about, but it seems to symbolize my dilemma. I'm not prepared to handle Nico Tacone and everything it might mean to go on a date with him.

I'm not even remotely prepared to be the girlfriend of a mafia boss. And I sure as hell shouldn't be screwing one.

This is a man who carries a gun in a holster under his arm. A man involved with crime and the underworld. A killer.

A knock sounds on the door.

Shit!

I'm still in my bra and underwear, fifteen outfits donned and discarded around the room.

"He's here," I whisper urgently into the phone.

"Tell him you don't feel good."

"But I'm a terrible liar."

"Just tell him—"

The keycard slides in the lock and the door swings open. Right. Because he has a key and he owns me now. And I've let this happen. Been giddy about it, actually.

Tacone takes in my lack of dress and shuts the door quickly behind him. His eyes glitter, dark and serious. He's in the same suit as this morning, finely tailored to fit over his large, powerful frame.

"You're not ready." He sounds disappointed, like I'm an errant employee who didn't follow instructions.

"I-I—I don't have anything to wear." I opt for the truth, sweeping my hand around the destroyed room where my discarded clothes hang from every surface.

His mouth twitches. He strolls slowly around the room, like he owns the place. Which makes sense because he does. He picks up a jean skirt and tosses it to me. "This and"—He finds a sleeveless blouse on the bed—"This."

"Listen," I say, my heart suddenly pounding hard. "I don't think this is going to work."

His eyes narrow. "Too late." He lifts his chin. "Put on the clothes, I have a surprise for you."

When I still hesitate, he comes and takes the blouse and pulls it over my head. "Come on. You'll like it, I promise."

I'm almost relieved to have the decision taken out of my hands. He's not giving me a choice, is he?

Except deep down, I'm pretty sure he'd let me off the hook if I were sincere. He knows when I'm bullshitting.

I pull on the jean skirt and my platform sandals, which make Nico give my legs an approving up and down look. He gives my ass a smack when I walk past him to the door. The burn and tingle has me blushing.

"What's the surprise?" I ask.

He smiles. "Dinner first. Then the surprise." He escorts me to the rooftop restaurant, the casino's fine dining establishment. I tug on my skirt as we enter, feeling underdressed.

"Stop it." He leans down and murmurs in my ear. "You look beautiful."

The staff scrambles to find us the best table in the house, one that overlooks the entire strip and yet is tucked away in a corner for privacy. He orders some Yamazaki whiskey I've never heard of and I ask for the house red. He shakes his head. "Bring her the 2003 Bannockburn Pinot."

"Of course, Mr. Tacone."

When I raise a brow, he winks. "It's good."

"You know your wines."

He shrugs his wide shoulders. "I make it my business to know everything that's served, spoken or happens in this casino."

A tingle of awareness pricks the base of my spine. The refrain that always returns plays in my head. This is a dangerous man. Never forget it.

I look at him, then survey the room. I don't even know what kind of conversation to make. Asking about his business probably isn't cool, considering the way he shook me down the day we met.

The next time my gaze flicks to his, it locks. He's staring at me with that burning intensity that makes my stomach somersault. "Tell me everything, Sondra Simonson. I want to know what makes you tick."

I'm not falling for flattery today. "You first," I dare. "I know nothing about you except you have a lot to hide and a thing for cleaning girls."

His lips twitch. "Not girls. Just you. And you're not a fucking cleaning girl."

"What am I then?"

I'm expecting some definition of our relationship, but he scowls.

"You're an art history professor who somehow fell down the trap door into my little corner of hell."

If he's trying to scare me again, it doesn't work. I've moved past his threats. I'm still here. I want to know the real Tacone now. "Tell me something real. Not about business. About you."

His eyebrows fly up. "Okay...I've got a brother visiting from Chicago who busts my balls. I'm counting the minutes until he leaves." He rubs a hand across his face. "That's just between you and me, of course."

"Older?"

"Yeah, of course. Thinks he's the family's boss."

"Because your dad's in jail." When Tacone looks at me sharply, I shrug. "I know how to Google *Tacone Crime Family*."

His face relaxes into a fleeting smile. "Yeah, exactly."

"Must be hard, all those alpha males in one family."

A laugh bursts out of him, deep and rich. The maître d' and waitstaff look over, surprised, like they didn't know he was capable of laughing. I become the object of curious stares.

"Yeah, I guess. I do like to be in charge. I'm the fourth son, so I knew I'd never inherit the kingdom. I think that's why I pushed so hard to get free of them. Or as free as I could. Out of state, my own operation. It was a goddamn necessity."

"So how many siblings altogether?"

"Five."

"Names? Order?"

His lips twitch. "You really want to know this shit?" When I nod, he smiles again. "Okay, pay attention." He holds up his hand to count on his fingers. "Junior is the

125

oldest. Then Paolo, then Gio. I'm next. Stefano is last. Alessia is the baby."

"Your mom was holding out for a girl."

He laughs again. "Exactly. Hard to believe the rest of us didn't break her, isn't it?"

I like the way his face goes soft when he talks about his mom. It strikes me as a good sign. A man who loves his mom will treat a woman right. At least that's what conventional wisdom says.

"She's here visiting, too. My brother's finding her a winter residence. I'd introduce you, but I like you too much to subject you to my family."

I would laugh, but his tone is a shade too dark.

Our drinks arrive and we order our food.

"Your turn. Tell me why you love art so much, *bambina*."

I smile. "Who can say why they love something? When I see beautiful art, it makes my heart yearn. Like I want to possess the beauty or the ingenuity."

"You ever want to be an artist?"

I shake my head. "No. I just love to study the history of it. It's fascinating to me."

"Who's your favorite artist?"

I take a sip of wine. "Too hard a question. I could tell you my favorite from each period?"

"All right." He watches me so intently, I shift in my seat. "Surrealist."

"It's cliché, but I have to say Picasso."

He smiles like I gave the right answer.

"Are you a fan?"

"Me?" He shrugs. "Never thought much about it. Not

sure I care one way or the other." His phone buzzes and he checks the text, then sends something back. It buzzes again.

He curses and pinches the bridge of his nose. "Sondra, baby—will you excuse me for five minutes?" He's already out of his seat. "Please don't leave. I really want to show you something after dinner." He waits, pinning me with a questioning look.

The fact that he suggests I'll leave tells me it will be more than five minutes. I don't relish the idea of sitting here by myself, but then again, it's an expensive restaurant with gourmet food. I might as well enjoy it. And I'd be a bitch to begrudge Nico for needing to leave. He has a whole freaking casino to run.

I nod. When he leaves, I pull out my phone to keep me company and the waiter brings just my food. My stomach knots when I see a text from a Reno number. I didn't program his name into my phone when I changed my number, but I know it's Tanner's. He must've finally found someone to give him my new number.

Sondra, this is urgent. You can keep the car, but I need something out of it.

The next text came a half hour later.

Seriously. It's really important.

Then one five minutes ago.

Like life or death important.

I look at the lobster on my plate and lose my appetite.

Crap. Tanner had drugs in the car. The knowing comes with the calmness of the eye of a storm. My DJ party boy ex peddled a little ecstasy. At least that's what I

127

knew. Sounds like he was into bigger deals than I understood.

And the car? The car is long gone. I had it towed to the wreckage yard. I mean, maybe he can find it and get back what he needs, but I doubt it.

∼

Nico

I'M DEALING with three idiot would-be coke dealers in my dungeon. Yes, my basement is a fucking dungeon, with an underground network of tunnels that lead out into the city. You might call them catacombs, because more than one body has been buried here.

They're kids. Young. Stupid. Easy to scare.

Security caught them moving powder in my nightclub. They could've called the cops, but I prefer to deal with this kind of shit in my own way. A little dose of fear goes a helluva lot farther than the threat of a badge.

I nod at my younger cousin Sal, who busts one of the guy's nose, then pulls his head up by the hair. All three of them have been worked over by my soldiers.

"This is Mr. Tacone, owner of the Bellissimo. He has something to say to you."

The kid is shitting himself. I walk over and look down my nose at him. "You think you can sell drugs in my club? In my casino?"

"I'm sorry, Mr. Tacone," the guy on the left babbles.

"W-we didn't know who you were. That you owned this place. We'll never come back."

I consider. I could make these boys my bitches and have them tithe to me from their profits, but they're too young and stupid. They wouldn't last long, anyway. I opt for the get out of town threat. "You have one day to leave my city. If we find you here again, you're dead. *Capiche?*"

"Yes, sir, yes, Mr. Tacone." All three babble their promises.

I nod to Sal and leave. I'm just grateful Junior didn't get a whiff of this or he'd be all over it, just for the drama. No, he's actually been out doing what he said he was doing—real estate shopping with our ma. She called me tonight to say they'd put an offer in on a place and were heading back to Chicago in the morning.

Normally I might stay and give this shit a bit more attention, but Sondra's upstairs, waiting for me. At least I hope she waited.

I sent Tony to find her cousin out on the floor and send her up to keep her company. I check my watch. *Fuck.*

It's been thirty minutes since I left her. She's probably finished dinner and dessert by now. It's crazy how much I care about whether she stuck around. How much I want to show her my surprise.

I walk as swiftly through the Bellissimo as I can, cursing the block-long floor plan that makes it nearly a mile to get back to the rooftop restaurant.

Sondra and Corey are still there, but I was right— they're already finished with dessert and are drinking coffee. And, of course, my mom and fucking brother are sitting just a few feet away.

I grind my teeth. *Cristo*, would it be too much for one thing to go right tonight?

I detour to my ma and brother's table and shower them with my most effusive host protocol. They eat it up, until Junior sees me shooting a glance at Sondra's table. Then his eyes narrow. He sees far too fucking much, my brother.

"If you'll excuse me, I have to greet some other guests, but my staff will give you everything you could possibly desire."

My ma offers her cheek for a kiss, but Junior just nods. I feel his eyes on me as I head to Sondra's table.

I have to get her out of here, because if I know my prick of a brother, he'll be sure to mention my fiancée if he suspects there's anything between Sondra and I.

Corey stands up when I get there, and walks toward me with a cool glance. I reach in my pocket and pull out a fifty-dollar chip to hand to her as we pass. She takes it without comment.

Sondra appears upset, though. She gets up and fusses with the strap of her purse.

I escort her out without touching her, because I don't want Junior or my ma drawing any conclusions. We walk in silence, a thin line of tension straining between us.

I'm not really one to say I'm sorry. I've done it more with this girl since I met her than I have in the entire last year. "I apologize—"

"It's all right," she says quickly.

That's when I realize something else is up.

We're outside the restaurant and I stop, pulling her around to face me. "What's bothering you?"

She shakes her head. "It's nothing."

I bristle and put a knuckle under her chin. *"Don't fucking lie to me."*

She pales and I close my eyes.

Cazzo.

I brought the violence of the basement back up with me. Sondra doesn't deserve my temper. My meanness. She doesn't deserve the darkness that is my life.

I tug her around to the bay of elevators and take one down to my suite, below. I wanted to show her my surprise, but it will have to wait. I need to know what's going on in her head.

The moment we get inside, I fold my arms across my chest.

"Talk."

She nibbles her lip and looks away.

"Sondra." I infuse my voice with authority. I know I shouldn't bully her, but it's in my blood.

"I might need your help. And I really hate to ask for it."

Relief sweeps through me. She has a problem that I can fix. This is what I do best. "You need money? It's yours." That's usually the kind of problem people ask me to solve. That or they need protection. Or require some kind of violent justice be served.

The misery on her face staggers my confidence. "What is it, *piccolina?* Just tell me."

"It's not for me. That's kind of the problem. It's not even for someone I care about, other than I don't want him to get killed."

And then my heart solidifies into a lump of hard concrete. This is about her ex.

"And his life is in danger because of me, so...I kinda feel responsible."

Violence pours into me like a storm. I want to kill her *stronzo* ex for having the goddamn audacity to even be born.

"Don't tell me this is about your fucking ex."

I already know it is.

Her shoulders slump. "I'm so sorry." Her voice is barely above a whisper.

I pace away from her. "You're so sorry for what?"

"For asking this of you."

And that's what puts me in a hard spot. I can't refuse her, even though it's for some other *figlio di puttana*. I shove my hands in my pockets to keep from fisting them, and rotate to face her. "What is it you need?"

"I might not need anything. I mean, he's going to come to Vegas to look for the car at the salvage yard."

I can't stand the way she fidgets with her purse strap, can't take her agitation.

"He had drugs stashed in it. I guess a lot. And he owes someone thirty thousand now."

I turn away as dark red anger floods my vision. My fist cracks through the drywall in front of me.

"Nico," she chokes. "Never mind. I'm sorry." When I turn back, I see tears tracking down her cheeks.

My brain goes haywire, wanting to inflict violence on the guy who made her cry, not computing it's me. After a breath, some other instinct kicks in and the need to comfort her sends me across the room. I want to pull her into my arms, to cup her face, and thumb away the tears, but I don't trust myself to touch her. Not when I'm so hot to hurt someone.

"You're crying over him?" I demand, too harshly.

To my surprise, she smacks my chest. "No, I'm crying over you." I somehow manage not to stagger back. Her words gut me. "I'm crying because you think I give a shit about him. Because of what I'm doing to our relationship asking for this."

And then I'm lost in relief. In gratitude. My hands are all over her, yanking her clothes off. I meld my mouth to hers and back her up against the wall. I have her skirt up, her panties pulled to the side and my finger strokes along her dewy slit. "What's our relationship, *bambi*?"

She stiffens, but I don't back off. I devour her mouth, screw one finger inside her. "What's our relationship? Are you saying you're my girl?"

"Nico," she whimpers, her head sliding along the wall as I push my finger in and out.

"Huh? Are you mine, Sondra?" I shove another finger in, fuck her with both of them. "You gonna accept that I own this pussy now? You give it to me any time I demand it?"

She clutches my forearms. Little sex cries come from her lips, but she's pushing me away. I know I'm going way too far, but I can't stop myself. I want to hear her say it. I want her to admit she's mine.

"Nico," she repeats my name.

"Say it, baby. You belong to me now. Say it and I'll help the *figlio di puttana*. So long as you promise never to talk to him again."

"I promise," she says quickly.

133

I withdraw my fingers and she gasps in surprise, her eyes opening and focusing on mine. "*Say it.*"

"I-I belong to you."

"Good girl." Pure power runs through me now. Like the adrenaline of a fight, of a kill. I pull a condom from my pocket and unbuckle my belt.

She watches me with glazed eyes, her chest still heaving from the finger fucking.

I make quick work of the condom and flatten her against the wall, shoving my dick between her legs.

She takes me, lifting one leg to draw me in.

"That's it, *piccolina*. Take every goddamn inch of me. This is the cock that owns you."

Her cries grow louder, her head rolling against the wall. The hole where my fist went through is just to her right, a reminder of what I've earned.

She wraps both legs around my waist, like she did in the shower and I get even deeper inside her. Wanting to fuck her so hard her teeth rattle, I carry her to the bedroom and lay her on the edge of the bed. Then I pound into her, my sanity slipping with each glorious thrust. I'm like a fucking gladiator, or a ruthless, rutting beast. I'm not thinking about her pleasure, not holding back from the violence with which I need to claim her.

One moment I think I could go all night, just dip my dick in her over and over again until the earth falls apart. And the next, I'm coming like a freight train.

I roar and slam deep.

Sondra screams and wraps her legs behind my back, using her heels to pull me even deeper. I come and come and come some more as her muscles squeeze my dick.

And then we break apart. I stagger to the bathroom to dispose of the condom.

When I come back, Sondra's sitting up, eyes wide and frightened. She stands and pulls down her skirt.

"Hey." I reach for her, but she turns away. I pull her back against my front, wrap my arms around her and hold her fast. "You're scared."

She draws in a long, shaky breath.

"Don't be scared of me, *piccolina*. I'm a dick. I say asshole things. Doesn't mean I don't respect you." I turn her to face me. She bursts into tears again and I go ice cold. What have I done? "I'm sorry." I cup the back of her head, lift her face to me. "Did I hurt you? Look at me, Sondra. Please? Did you feel like I forced you?"

"No." She answers immediately, which gives me some measure of relief.

"What is it, then?"

She wipes her tears. "It was just intense."

I pull her right up against my body, hold her tight. "Hell, yeah, it was intense. For me, too."

She blinks those big blue eyes at me. "Why was it intense for you?"

I consider for a moment. I want to answer truthfully, but the answer scares the shit out of me.

Because she cares. She cares about me. And our relationship.

And this is exactly why I shouldn't be messing with sweet Sondra Simonson. Because I'm not even remotely available. Even if I wasn't promised to another, I can't devote the time and attention to her that she deserves. Just look how poorly tonight went—

our date ruined by the kind of mishap that happens hourly around here.

Sondra's already giving me her heart, and I'd be the worst kind of *stronzo* to take it.

The very worst.

~

Sondra

"SO YOU'LL HELP?"

Nico grimaces, but he nods. "I'll help *you*."

I clutch his arm. "You won't hurt him?"

His nostrils flare. "I can't fucking stand you begging me on his behalf, *bambi*."

I can't really stand it, either. Tanner shouldn't be screwing up my relationship with Nico. But I feel responsible for taking the car. I knew when I did it, it was the wrong thing to do, but I wanted to punish him. But not with death.

I drop my forehead against his chest and he strokes the back of my neck. I still can't believe such a powerful man is so into me, but knowing he's willing to give me this means everything.

"I won't hurt him," he mutters, disgust registering in his voice. "But if it costs me thirty large, I'm going to take payment out on your ass."

I jerk my head up to read his expression and find him smirking. My butt clenches at the threat. Does he mean more spanking? Because I pretty much loved every time he's done it.

"Give me the details on the car. I'll send my guys over there tonight to find the drugs." I tell him everything I can about the car and the salvage yard and he gets on his phone and barks orders. When he hangs up, I thank him.

"Do I still get my surprise?"

He barks out that booming laugh and it seems to surprise even him. "Yes, *piccolina.* Come on." He grabs my hand and suddenly we're headed out the door of his suite, back into the elevator. He uses his keycard to punch in a number, which means we're going to a private floor. I'm intrigued.

He pushes me up against the elevator wall and claims my mouth, not stopping the kiss until the doors open and I squirm. Then he turns on a dime and tugs me out of the elevator, moving briskly through what appear to be management offices. We arrive at a door flanked by two security guards.

"Mr. Tacone." They nod their deferential greetings. Nico presses his thumb to the pad, then brings his eye level for a retinal scan.

High tech.

The heavy door unclicks and one of the guards pulls it open for us.

We step into a giant, room-sized safe. Carts of neatly bundled cash make my eyes bug out, but Nico heads over to a cabinet, which he opens. He pulls out a rectangular object draped in black cloth.

Art.

I rush to his side, my heart already beating faster. I

know before he uncovers it it's a Picasso. Even so, a shudder of pleasure, of recognition, runs through me. It's from his blue period, of a woman sitting in a chair.

"Nico," I breathe. "Where did you get this?"

He doesn't look at the painting at all—he's only watching my reaction to it.

"I occasionally collect debt payment in the form of fine art and gems."

"Do you know what this is worth?"

"I had it valued." He says this casually, like the ten million-dollar painting isn't what interests him.

"What's the name of this one? I've never seen pictures of it."

"*Woman in Chair.*" He reaches in the cabinet and pulls out another painting, then another. He unveils four Picassos, one Rembrandt, two Rothkos and a Renoir.

I'm practically swoony by the time I've examined them all up close. "You should have these on display. Set up the Bellissimo Museum or something."

Nico has his hands in his pockets. He's standing back, observing me, like I'm the rare and valuable masterpiece. "I could. I'd have to invest in heavy security. Plus, then everyone and their brother knows how much wealth I have sitting around here."

"True, but it could be a draw. It might set your casino apart as something really special The must-see of Las Vegas." I gasp as an idea occurs to me. "You could make the whole place about art. Go with Italian artists and decorate the different towers in different periods."

Nico's eyes glitter and his lips curl into a smile. "That's an idea, yes."

He wraps the paintings back up, one by one and replaces them. When he takes my hand to lead me out, he says, "You really love them."

My mouth falls open. "How can you not?"

He chuckles. "For me they're just a different form of currency. A diversification of my portfolio. For you, they're like—I don't know—living beings."

I laugh, because that's exactly how I see art. "Yes. Incredible beings. They should be on display."

He leads me back out to the elevator. "I'll make you a deal. I'll set up a museum—redecorate the Bellissimo if you direct and curate it."

I stop mid-stride. "Really? You'd let me curate?"

"Of course. Who the fuck else would I hire?"

I throw my arms around him because those paintings are already in my soul. Already calling to me, begging to be shown, to be celebrated. "Thank you. I'd love to."

He smiles down at me. "You're happy." He sounds half-surprised, half-satisfied.

I kiss his stubbled jaw. "So happy."

"Good."

He takes me back up to his place, but when he opens the door, he ushers me in, but doesn't close it. "I have work to do, but I want you to sleep in my bed tonight."

He doesn't ask. It's an order.

"What if I say no?" I ask, testing.

He raises a brow. "Why would you?"

Good point. Why would I? Just to prove he doesn't own me? Didn't I just promise he did?

I guess I need to know how deep I'm in. Would he let

139

me go if I said no? Or would he hold Tanner over my head? How real is this?

I take it back—I don't want to know. I want to stick my head deep in the sand and enjoy what I have. An incredible new job opportunity.

And a man who thinks I'm the cat's meow.

And the fact that he's a dangerous criminal can just get swept under the rug for the moment.

"I don't have my toothbrush here."

Nico's lips twitch. "I'll have one brought up for you. I need to go and I don't want you running around the casino by yourself."

I roll my eyes and he cocks a stern brow. "Indulge me, *cucciola mia*. I need to know you're up here keeping my bed warm with this hot little body."

He pulls me against him and I melt into his hard-muscled form.

"What's *cucciola*?"

"Pet. I called you *my pet*."

That seems a fitting name for a woman he thinks he owns.

I swallow down my nerves. He respects me. He just created a dream job for me. I don't need to be afraid.

Or do I?

ico

I ENTER my suite around five in the morning. Like every night this week, Sondra's in my bed sleeping. Where she belongs.

My guys found the drugs in her car—a half pound of molly, which has a street value of more than $30K. They delivered it to her asshole ex with a mild beat-down and the warning to never contact Sondra again. Problem solved. I'm not even pissed anymore, because I got to be her hero.

I stand in the doorway and look at her, so beautiful, her expression sweet in slumber. If I were a decent man, I'd let her sleep. But I can't fucking sleep until I've put my dick into her, so I take off my clothes and climb over her.

She murmurs something in her sleep, her knees parting to make room for me. My cock is harder than stone, already leaking for her. I've been waiting for this moment all fucking night, but I had three private games to manage that took my attention.

Sondra's wearing a tank top and a pair of pink satin panties. I tug up her tank and feast on one nipple.

"Nico." She weaves her fingers into my hair, her eyelids fluttering as she wakes.

I love hearing my name on her lips. I thumb her pussy over the triangle of silk covering it. "You're wearing panties in my bed, baby."

She smiles. "Oops."

I pause for a beat, trying to work out if she means what I think she does. Last night, in a fit of filthy talk, I told her I expected to find her pussy bare when I come to bed.

"Are you hoping for a spanking?"

Her grin grows wider and she arches into me.

I yank down the panties. "You'll be punished for that, *amore*."

She rolls her hips on the bed. I flip her over to her stomach and slap her ass. It's so spankable, but I'm low on patience tonight. I smack her cheeks a half-dozen times and then knock her legs wide. "Spread 'em for me, angel. I'm harder than steel for you and I have been all night." I grab a pillow and shove it under her hips to give me a better angle. "No foreplay for you, naughty girl. You'll have to take my cock exactly how I want to give it to you."

She raises her ass. Oh hell, a few slaps won't kill her. I meant to keep them light, but the second my hand connects with her ass, I want more. I smack her harder, louder. Four more. She moans, wantonly. "I gave you one simple rule. Keep this pussy bare for me." I push her ass cheeks wide. "Makes me think you wanted my punishment."

She makes an *mmm* sound.

I grip her hair and lift her head. "Did you?"

"Yes!" she gasps.

I release her hair and massage her scalp to take away the sting.

"Maybe I should fuck your ass to teach you a lesson." She goes rigid, which wasn't what I was going for. Still, I pull her cheeks wide and bump the head of my cock against her anus to make her squeal.

"No, please," she whimpers.

"Are you going to be a good girl?"

"Yes, sir."

Oh *Madonna*. I love it when she calls me *sir*. I roll on a condom and push into her without preamble. She's already slick with her own juices, but she cries out. I stop at the hilt and bite her neck. "Okay, baby?"

"Yes. Yes, Nico."

Damn. I'm one stroke in and already need to come, just because she said my name. "That's right, baby. Say my name. Whose cock are you going to take?"

She moans and even through the condom I can tell her pussy got wetter. "Yours. God, yes."

I mutter several curses in Italian as I continue to plow into her. She's so soft, so willing. So fucking responsive. It's like our bodies were made for each other's. I need her with an intensity that humbles me.

This is what drives me to act like a possessive asshole. To want to own her, control her. I know it's not right, but

I can't stop myself. And while it turns her on, I also know it scares her. Which also turns her on. I'm learning everything that makes my little art historian tick.

I push her ass cheeks apart to give her the sensation of my loins against her asshole and she cries out, excitement wavering in her voice.

"This ass belongs to me, doesn't it, *bella*?"

She moans with each quick pant, a tapestry of sound to accompany the slap of flesh against flesh.

"Say you need this cock, baby. Say you need it as much as I need your tight little pussy."

"I need it," she pants. "I need it so badly."

It's all over for me. My eyes roll back in my head. I ride her like my life depends on it, like if I don't fuck her hard enough, neither one of us will survive. She fists the bed sheets, screaming with each thrust.

My balls draw up painfully tight, thrusts become erratic. "Come for me, angel. Come as fucking hard as I'm going to."

I release, burying myself deep inside her and climaxing so forcefully I nearly black out. I'm gone for a few moments, and then I realize my weight is on her and I roll off, pulling her to spoon against my front, our bodies still connected.

I finger one nipple, gently squeezing and tugging. "Baby, you have no idea what you do to me." The orgasm has me grateful. I want to offer her money, gifts, anything she'll take. But I don't want her to feel cheap, either. I know it's a sensitive point for her. Every day I thank the stars I figured out a position she loves that I can pay her to do. "What can I do for you? Tell me what you need."

She goes quiet for too long, which makes me itchy. Something's on her mind. Something she's not sure how to say.

I pull out of her and throw the condom in the wastebasket beside the bed. She half-rolled to her back, but her head's still turned away from me. I roll her to face me. "Tell me, baby. I'm not making you happy. What is it?"

She blinks for a moment, then draws a breath. "Am I your girlfriend, Nico? Your booty call? What am I to you?"

I lean up on one elbow, trying not to show my alarm. This is the conversation I've dreaded. Can Nico Tacone have a girlfriend?

"What do you want to be?" I stroke her hair back from her face, but she jerks away, irritation in the movement.

"Are you asking if there's someone else, baby? You have to know there's not. You think I could come this hard if I were fucking another woman?"

She drags her lip through her teeth. "No," she says slowly. "I don't think that. It's one of the things I like about you. You make me feel so desirable. If I had one hint there was another woman, I'd be out of here in a heartbeat. After Tann—"

I raise my brows and a warning finger. "Don't say his name."

"Well, you know what happened with him. I'm never doing that again."

Alarm bells are going off in the back of my head. She's telling me something important. She's not going to tolerate infidelity. Which isn't a problem.

Except for my fucking marriage contract.

Twenty-two years ago, my father made an arrangement with Giuseppe Pachino to permanently combine our two families. Because they are both old-world men, neither balked at the idea of binding a ten-year-old boy to a newborn girl without their consent. In fact, they celebrated the return to the old customs, their wisdom and our combined prosperous future. Giuseppe has no sons, and so my father, I believe, thought he was providing me with the chance to one day be boss of a powerful family. He didn't realize I'd make my own chances. Become boss on my own terms.

But the two crime families have operated with mutually beneficial terms ever since.

I know very little about Jenna Pachino. I've avoided her like the plague. I kinda figured she must be as horrified by the contract as I am and would take my absence as a relief.

But I haven't cancelled the contract. Only my father can do that, and he's sitting in jail. And until now, it didn't really matter to me.

And I shouldn't consider it now. Because—

Fuck. I've been quiet too long. Sondra's face closes.

"There's no one else," I say fiercely, to counteract whatever conclusion she's drawn.

Except it's a fucking lie, isn't it?

"I don't think you want to be permanently bound to me, though, baby. Do you know what I am?"

Even in the filtered light of the city coming through the windows I see her pale. Her mouth cinches up.

I grip her jaw. "I will fucking possess you. I'll claim you for life. But I'd be condemning you to eternity with the devil. Crime is in my blood. Violence is behind my name.

I've tried to distance myself. I try to keep my hands clean over here, running a legit business, paying taxes on the money we make. But I'll never be free of it. And I don't want to take you down with me."

Her eyes fill with tears and she rolls away. I catch her by the waist as she sits up, her back to me.

"Please. Don't go." What am I asking her? My brain races, trying to come up with some solution, some compromise that will keep her in my bed. "Give me just a little more time with you. I'm not ready to give you up. Stay. Get my museum up and running. Redecorate the casino. Then I promise I'll let you go."

She turns to look back at me. I see longing and pain reflected in those beautiful blue eyes.

"I never beg, baby. That's how much you mean to me."

She doesn't turn around. "What am I agreeing to?" Her voice sounds hoarse. "Just sex?"

"No." My voice is harsh. Her question makes sense. Sex is all I've had time to give her, and yet the idea of her suggesting that's all I want pisses me off. I need so much more than sex. I crave possessing her—body, mind, soul. "Girlfriend, if that's how you want to define it. I want your time and attention, too."

She gives a snort and I realize my lack of presence has been felt.

"I'm sorry I've been so busy, angel. I will make time for you. I promise."

Even I hear the emptiness of the promise. Because it's one I'm not sure how to deliver. This casino takes up twenty-three out of the twenty-four hours in a day, and the remaining hour it's still in my thoughts, which is why I can't sleep without fucking Sondra like a raging bull.

But if that's what she needs, I'll figure it the fuck out. I always do.

"Come back to bed, *bella*. You know I can't sleep without you beside me."

She allows me to tug her down to the mattress and wrap my longer body around hers. Within a few moments, her breath slows and she falls asleep. Me—I'm awake for an hour before I finally give up on sleep and go take a shower.

~

Sondra

"YOU'RE FALLING FOR HIM." Corey kicks her legs in the Bellissimo pool. We're sitting on the side near the faux boulders and man-made waterfall, a week after Nico begged me to stay and promised to make time for me. It hasn't happened.

"No, I'm not."

"Bullshit. If you weren't, you'd be perfectly happy to stay with him, let him pay for all your expenses and have great sex until you figure out your next move. But you're not. You want something more."

I drop into the pool, keeping my arms above the water. The knot of dread tightening in my belly tells me she's dead on. I want something more and Nico can't give it.

He's made that abundantly clear. Although I'm not sure if he's telling me the whole story.

After being lied to and cheated on more times than I care to admit, an alarm bell is going off somewhere in my subconscious. But maybe that's just me being paranoid. Maybe I'm too damaged from my past mistakes to even know a relationship worth fighting for when it bites me in the ass.

"Well, something more isn't on the docket." I walk through the water, letting it cool my skin, warm from the sun.

"So you need to figure out what you want. If you need to protect your heart, you should go now. Or you could decide to just get everything you can out of this experience—great sex, resume building, publicity, a story to tell your grandkids—and ride it out until the museum's set up, like he suggested."

"Yeah." I wish it were that easy. But my heart is totally in play. And it's already showing signs of damage. And yet no part of me is willing to walk away yet.

I'm not sure why not—because it's so intoxicating to be desired, I guess. And I might tell myself he's all talk—this is the smooth-talking Romeo who has me under his spell, except I see first-hand how well he sleeps after we've had sex. He looks ten years younger afterward, the lines in his face easing, the light coming back into his eyes.

It's egotistical to believe, but I think he needs me.

I climb out of the pool and wrap a towel around my waist. "I'm going to go work on the museum stuff."

Corey pulls her feet out of the water and slips them

into flip flops. "If he promised to make more time for you and he hasn't delivered, you should demand it from him. That was the arrangement you had."

Demanding anything from Nico Tacone is a big, fat laugh.

"Or you could just show up on the floor tonight in a sexy dress and watch him flip out." A wicked grin plays around Corey's lips.

I pause in the act of picking up my swim bag. Nico's jealous enough that he didn't want me dealing cards or cleaning anyone else's room. It probably wouldn't take much to tweak him into action. "That *would* guarantee a reaction."

Corey smiles. "I have the perfect dress you can borrow. A slinky red wrap-around. Wear it with a pair of fuck-me pumps and he'll forget all about work for the night."

It's a better idea than the one I've been trying—working as hard as Nico to distract myself from my thoughts of why this relationship is all wrong.

"Let's go get the dress."

ico

I'M an asshole because I promised to treat Sondra like a girlfriend and not a fucktoy, and then I haven't had a goddamn minute during the waking hours to treat her right.

I pick up my phone and call Stefano, my younger brother. He and I are tight—close in age and of a similar mindset. He's been in the old country, working with our great uncle.

"Nico, *come va?*" he answers.

I get right to the point. "I need you."

Stefano swears. "What is it?"

"No, no. Nothing bad. My operation has grown too big. I can't work enough hours in the day, and I need someone to share the load. I need you, specifically."

Stefano's quiet for a moment. "Tony's not enough?"

151

"Tony can't do everything. And he's not my brother. I pay him well, but I can't share the kingdom with him. Dad wouldn't allow it."

"Yeah, okay. I'll talk to *Zio*. I'm sure he can let me go if you really need me."

"I do. I need you to head up security. That way I can focus on continued growth. Call me back and let me know when you can come."

"I will." I'm about to hang up, when he says, "Nico?"

I put the phone back to my ear.

"What prompted this?"

"What do you mean?"

"Are you sick? Did something happen?"

I blow out a breath. This is why I need Stefano. He's fucking perceptive. "It's a woman."

Stefano lets out a surprised bark of laughter. "No shit?"

"Yeah. And I'm working twenty hours a day and she's gonna walk."

"You're serious about this woman?"

Everything in my chest tightens because I know what Stefano's next question will be. I try to head it off by saying, "I'm not sure."

"Bullshit. You're serious. What about Jenna Pachino?"

"Yeah, I don't know. I need to cancel that contract, I guess."

"Have you talked to Dad?"

"Not yet."

"Well, you'd better do it soon. He's not gonna want any surprises. Does he know you're calling me back?"

I want to put my fist through the wall. I hate being fucking bound by my family. "No."

"Talk to him first, Nico. I don't want to get in the middle of your shit pile."

"I'll fucking talk to him!" I snap. "You get on a fucking plane to Vegas."

"*Si, signore.*" Stefano's voice is dry, but I know he won't hold a real grudge over me being a dick.

I start to hang up without a goodbye, but then I bring the phone back to my ear. "*Grazie, Fratello.*"

"Good to hear from you, Nico. I'm glad you found someone." Stefano's voice has gone soft. "And you're still a *stronzo.*"

Yes, I am an asshole. "Always."

He snorts and hangs up and I'm left smiling into the phone, which is about as uncharacteristic for me as doing a jig in a leprechaun suit.

I head out on the floor, where I have at least six fucking issues to take care of, in addition to wooing three big spender whales.

I stop short.

Sondra sits at the bar in a slinky red dress, her shapely legs punctuated with a pair of sexy black heels. She pulled her hair up into a sophisticated French twist and is drinking a martini.

As if that isn't enough to absorb, there's a guy sitting next to her, leaning in and making conversation.

I'm going to kill the fucker.

"Mr. Tacone, Jeff Blue has been asking to speak with you about a private game." One of my managers is at my elbow.

Merda.

No, maybe it's for the best. I need to calm down. I can't go rip the guy off the barstool and smash his head in just for talking to my girl.

What is she doing?

I move swiftly toward Jeff Blue and force myself to act civil. This is a man who drops ten to fifty thousand a night when he's in my establishment. I make time for him when he comes.

I don't even know what I say to him, because the whole time my eye is on the sexy blonde at the bar. Before I pull away, though, the other whale joins us. He recognizes Jeff and wants in on a private game.

Fuck.

Private games are great. I make a killing. But they require a helluva lot of security and handholding. This is why I need Stefano here.

I'm gnawing through my leash when some other asshole sits on the other side of Sondra. She rotates in her chair and sees me, but all I get is a fucking smile and a fresh crossing of her stocking-clad legs.

Oh shit.

She's jerking me on purpose.

I blink, my mind going to white fuzz for a moment. I'm less frantic than I am pissed now.

Tony comes over to tell me about a new fucking emergency with an attempted scam in the back room.

I step away from the whales and yank him to the side. "Get Sondra out of here and in my suite now. If I see another fucking guy talking to her, I'm gonna lose my shit."

"Got it, boss. Leo and Sal are in the back room dealing with the con. You want me to come there when I'm done?"

"No, I'll need you on the private game as soon as I get it arranged."

"Understood."

I leave without looking back at Sondra again, because if I do, someone's going to lose their teeth.

Sondra

THIS WAS A HORRIBLE IDEA. I thought the ploy worked for a brief moment, when I sensed Nico's stare burning through my back, but he never came over, and when he left, he looked pissed.

And now his strong-arm is heading my way.

Tony steps up and looks at the guys sitting on either side of me. "Get lost."

One of them sputters with anger, the other slinks away like a stray dog caught stealing food.

"Do you want me to go?" Angry man demands.

I nod. "Yeah, you'd better."

He puffs up his chest. "Are you afraid of this guy?"

"Really. You should go. It was nice talking to you." I make my voice polite but firm. The guy is drunk enough to do something stupid, and I definitely don't want any kind of violence on my hands. "I'm fine."

He frowns, but when Tony takes a menacing step forward, decides to cut his losses and leave.

"Boss wants you upstairs, in his suite."

Oh, now that raises my hackles. "Excuse me?" He didn't even have the fucking time to come over and talk to me himself? And now he's sending me up to his suite? Bullshit.

Tony holds his hands up, palms out. "Hey, I don't want to be in the middle of a lover's spat. I have orders to get you up there. Nico has five fires burning or I'm sure he'd be over here himself."

Hearing about Nico's stress dampens my anger. Is it really fair of me to attempt to draw his attention away from his business?

Then again, is it fair for him to treat me like he owns me and order me around?

Tony leans an elbow on the bar beside me. "Listen. You're making my job tough here. If I touch you, Nico will have my balls. But I also have my orders. So what's it going to take to get you out of here and upstairs to the boss' suite?"

I fold my arms across my chest. "Information."

He lifts a brow. "Like what?"

What am I doing? Do I even want the answers to my questions?

"Am I..." What am I going to say? Special? His only one?

Tony cocks his head like he's trying his best to interpret crazy female.

"Am I his usual type?"

Tony blinks, surprise flitting over his face. He loops an

arm around my elbow. "Come on. Let me take you out of here and I'll tell you everything you want to know."

Mollified, I hop off the barstool and allow him to escort me to the private elevators. Once we're alone, he releases my elbow and faces me. "No. You're not his usual type. You're pretty fucking far from his usual type."

I'm not sure whether to be relieved or disappointed.

"You're the only woman he's wanted to screw—pardon my crudeness—more than once the entire time I've known him, which is since we were kids. So I don't know what he's told you, but I'd say you're pretty damn special to him."

Warmth seeps into my chest and my anger evaporates. "Yeah?"

Tony nods. "Yeah. And don't think every fucking person who works for him isn't grateful you're helping him sleep. He was hell on wheels to manage for a while there."

We arrive on Nico's floor and he escorts me to the door. "You gotta key?"

I fish the keycard out of the little evening purse I borrowed from Corey. "Yep. Thanks."

He waits until I open the door before he leaves.

"Good night, Tony."

"Good night, yourself, Ms. Simonson."

Ms. Simonson. I've definitely moved up in the casino world.

I go inside and pace around Nico's place. It could be hours and hours before he comes. It will probably be the usual 4:30 a.m. alarm cock wake up. That thought brings a weight crushing down on my chest. Too much feels unresolved, up in the air. I don't see how I'll sleep until we talk.

Fortunately, it's not too long. Nico comes in forty-five minutes later while I'm watching *Saturday Night Live* on the television. He still appears pissed.

I turn off the TV and stand up. He stands near the door, shoves his hands in his pockets and regards me.

The fact that he doesn't come closer sends my stomach plummeting. Usually he's all over me the minute he sees me.

"Sondra. You disrespected me down there."

My breath leaves me. *Disrespected.* Crap. This is an alpha male with a full-on mafia ego. Respect means everything.

I try to draw on my anger from earlier. He disrespected me, too. He hasn't made time for me, didn't even bother to come over, and treated me like a possession. I square my shoulders and open my mouth.

He holds up a hand before I can speak. "I know I let you down this week. I'm working on a fucking solution. But if you have a problem with me, you come and talk to me about it. You don't fucking make a fool out of me in my own club."

My heart sinks even further. "I wasn't making a fool—"

He holds up his hand again to silence me. "Never again."

My pussy clenches at the steel in his voice. Wow. A full-on Nico Tacone scolding. It's one part humiliating, two parts exciting. I'm definitely wired wrong because I find an angry mob boss thrilling.

He walks to the bar and pours himself a drink. "I have shit to do," he mutters, his back turned. "You should go to your own room tonight. I won't be here before daylight." He walks out on the balcony without looking back.

My heart's on the floor. He's angrier than I thought. I need to fix things before I go—I'm not about to leave on this note. Not when my emotions are on edge, my hormones are raging and Nico's still mad.

I follow him out.

He sinks into a seat and stares out at the night.

"Nico—"

"Not tonight, baby." His voice is clipped, tight.

I stand in front of him, blocking his view. "Nico."

In a quick, irritated move, he pulls me face down over his lap and lands nine quick hard smacks on my ass. The spanks hurt, but I'm more excited than anything else. This is a realm I'm familiar with. Him touching me, being a little too rough.

And it seems to change something in him, too. The moment the flurry of spanks stop, he's squeezing and palming my ass in that possessive way of his. He slides his hand up inside my dress and rubs between my legs. My panties are already damp and he growls when he feels them.

"Stand up and take off your panties for your spanking, baby." His voice is gravelly and rough. All the tightness is gone.

He helps me up and I shimmy out of my panties and lie back over his lap. This is sex, now. Nico's anger is gone and the current of lust runs between us, as strong as always. He slides one large palm up the back of my leg, dragging the hem of Corey's red dress with it. I'm wearing black thigh-high stockings with a seam up the back and bows at the top and Nico growls when he gets the full view of them.

Some of the anger returns to his voice, though. "Who did you wear these for?" He smacks my ass, hard.

"For you!" I yelp immediately.

He massages away the sting. "They better be for me." Another smack and massage. "My jealousy is a dangerous thing, baby. Don't ever play that game with me again." He tightens his grip around my waist and starts spanking. It's a real spanking—hard and fast. Unrelenting. My breath leaves me and rushes back in. I jerk and squirm because it's suddenly not so sexy. It hurts. A flash of real fear runs through me. How far will he take this?

"I'm sorry!" I cry out.

He stops immediately and rubs. "Show me, baby." His voice is low and rough again. He releases my waist.

I understand what he means and slide off his lap to the floor in front of him. He grabs the cushion from the seat beside him and nudges me up to cushion my knees. I'm eager to please. I don't think I've ever been so excited about giving a blowjob in my life. I unbuckle his belt and open his trousers to release his thick erection.

He watches me with heavy-lidded eyes as I lick around the head. My butt still stings from the spanking, which makes this servile all the hotter. I'm paying penance with my tongue, with my lips, my mouth. I take him deep and his thighs tense, knees shooting wider. I cup his balls and massage behind them, looking for the sensitive area between the balls and the anus.

I switch my hand, jacking him in a tight fist and moving my mouth lower to teabag him.

"Oh fuck!" Nico's hand tangles in my hair, knocking down my French twist. *"Madonna. Cristo. Dio.* What are you doing to me?"

I love the heady power that surges through me, knowing how much pleasure I'm giving him. I suck the other ball, lick the seam of his scrotum.

When I return to engulf his cock in my mouth, he surges forward in the chair, shoving it down my throat as he holds the back of my head captive. I choke, but don't stop sucking. I move up and down over his cock, taking him into the pocket of my cheek, then to the back of my throat. I've never been good at deepthroating, but for Nico I want to try. I slow down and relax my muscles.

He tightens his fist in my hair and groans. The string of Italian curses fuels my desire. I pick up my speed, bobbing over his cock, using my fist, too, so it feels like I'm taking his full length.

"Sondra. *Fuck!* Sondra." He comes down my throat.

I swallow. It's my first time not gagging, and I'm pretty damn proud of myself. It doesn't hurt that Nico's roar still echoes off the building. I continue to roll my tongue along the underside of his cock, sucking him dry. My clit pulses in time with my heartbeat. My ass is still hot and twitchy.

I need sex, desperately.

~

Nico

SONDRA'S SURRENDER leaves me utterly transformed. Maybe it's this quality in her all along that entranced me. The way she yields, makes herself vulnerable. To *me*— Nico Tacone—the guy most everyone cowers from.

Even when I bark, she stays soft.

She fucking stood up and took off her panties for my punishment. After I inexcusably lost my temper and smacked her ass in anger.

I'm humbled by her. Humbled and grotesquely empowered at the same time. Because I'm not about to give up the control she handed over to me. I'm taking this all the way.

"Come here, *bambi*." I lift her off her knees and sit her on my lap, facing away. "Open for me." I pull her thighs open and drape them over mine, so she's spread wide.

She leans back against me, her head falling onto my shoulder. Her breath rises and falls quickly and her skin is warm and soft. I slide my hands up her inner thighs, dragging the red dress with them. I palm her pussy.

She lets out a breathy sigh.

"I'll bet this pussy needs some attention," I murmur in her ear, giving her clit a light slap.

She shivers. "Yes, please."

Have I mentioned how much I fucking love it when she says *please*?

I slap her pussy again. It's wet, swollen. I dip my middle finger into her and she squirms against it, trying to work me in deeper.

I pump my digit in and out of her a few times, then stop. "I'm not sure I'm going to let you get off, though."

She whimpers.

"Do you think you deserve to come, angel?"

She goes still and I fear I've gone too far. But then she uses the most adorable pleading voice. "Please, Nico?"

I pump again. "Fuck. It's damn near impossible for me to deny you anything when you beg me in that sexy little voice, *bambi*."

"Please fuck me."

Oh Christ. My cock is already getting hard again. I'm going to lose this battle. But I play hardball with her. "Oh, I'm going to fuck you, angel." I slap her pussy. "I'm going to fuck you good. I'm going to fuck that tight little virgin ass of yours."

She goes still again, and I know she's scared. I nip her ear. "Don't worry," I murmur. "I'll make it good. I promise, baby."

I wait until she exhales and the tension in her muscles ease and then I lift her from my lap and stand up. "Go take off your dress and lie face down on my bed."

It's a test. If she doesn't do it, I'm not gonna push. I'm not that much of an asshole. But I do think I can make her like it. She cuts her eyes to me, then toddles toward the bedroom on unstable legs.

Victory makes my cock punch out hard again. I follow her to the bedroom and find a bottle of lube. I haven't had to use it with her—she seems to be constantly wet for me —but I'm glad I have it.

She obeys me, stripping off her dress and lying down on the bed, wearing only a black lace bra and the pair of sexy black stockings with a seam up the back.

"God*damn* that's a beautiful sight."

She turns her head to the side to look at me and her

gaze is almost shy—so shockingly vulnerable it makes my heart squeeze. I grab both the pillows from the bed and lift her hips. "Put these under you, angel and spread your sexy thighs."

I crawl up between her legs and pull her asscheeks apart. Lick a long line from her clit to her anus.

She mewls and shivers. I repeat the action, then give one cheek a smack. Her ass is still pink from the spanking I gave her, which shouldn't turn me on so much, but it does. I want to give her everything she needs. Make this the best possible intro to anal. I lube up her ass and my finger and start slow, massaging over her anus, penetrating her and working the tight ring of muscles open. I talk to her the whole time, soothing her, praising her. "That's it, baby. Open for me. Relax and let me in. Good girl."

When I work up to pumping my finger in her, she whimpers and slides a hand between her legs to rub her clit.

"That's it, angel. Take what you need. I'm going to fuck this sexy ass of yours now." I put on a condom and lube the hell out of it, then press the head of my cock at her entrance. "Take a deep breath."

Her back and ribs widen as she draws in her breath.

"Now exhale."

When she obeys, I ease in, feeding my length, inch by inch.

Her moan raises in pitch, but she doesn't tighten against me, doesn't resist. "Good girl. Take my big cock in your ass. This is what happens when you've been a naughty girl."

She moans louder, a wanton sound that I take as a green light. I fill her, all the way to the hilt, then ease back and fuck her again.

"Nico," she pants. "Oh my God."

"I know, baby. You're getting your ass fucked by the man who owns you." I know I'm an asshole, but I *have* to possess this woman, to own her, keep her, claim and dominate her. Especially after she made me watch her flirt with those fuckers downstairs.

I pound her ass, thoroughly fuck her until her cries take on a high pitched, panicked sound. "Please," she begs. "Please, oh please, oh please."

I already came once, so I could go on forever, but I know she's desperate to climax. I close my eyes and let the pleasure surge through me. My balls tighten up. I lower my hips to rest on her ass and rock in and out while I work my hand under her hips. Her fingers are frantic between her legs, but I knock them out of the way and sink three of mine into her wet channel. She's sopping— as juicy as I've ever felt a woman—and so swollen and slick.

"I'm going to come in your ass, baby, and when I tell you it's time, you're going to come all over my fingers. *Capiche?*"

"Yes! Please, Nico," she sobs.

The urgency of her need sends me over the cliff. My hips snap and I fuck her a few more times before I come again.

"*Now*, baby."

Her entire body convulses, pussy fluttering around my fingers, anus tightening almost painfully around my cock.

165

It must hurt her, too, because she cries out and her muscles go slack, surrendering once more.

"That's it, baby. Good girl." I kiss her neck. "You took it so well. Did you like your first ass-fucking?"

She doesn't answer and a little ball of dread starts building in my solar plexus. I ease out of her and throw the condom in the trash by the bed. "I'll be right back," I murmur and quickly wash my hands in the bathroom. The urgency to return to her is almost overwhelming.

She hasn't moved since I left her, she's still collapsed over the pillows, her ravished ass on display.

"Look at me, *piccolina*." I roll her over.

She doesn't seem to want me to see her face, because she lunges up for me, wrapping her arms tightly around my neck.

I hold her tight, petting her hair, kissing her temple. "Tell me you're okay, baby."

She nods against my neck. "I'm okay." Her voice is ragged.

"I need to see you."

Her arms tighten around my neck.

"Angel." I lower her back to the bed and roll to my side so we're facing one another. "Look at me."

She gradually releases her grip on my neck.

I cradle her face in one palm, run my thumb over her cheekbone. "I love you, Sondra."

I didn't mean to say it. I had no idea those words were going to come out of my mouth. But they're true. They're real. They're the best honesty I've ever known.

Her eyes fly wide and she studies me, like she's looking for some sign I mean it. Like she's afraid to believe me.

I feel the brakes slamming in my own chest. I'm leading her on. I'm not even *available* for this woman, but it's too late. I've said it, and I'm not taking it back.

"Don't say it back," I tell her. "I know it doesn't change things. It's just what came out when I saw your angelic face."

"So you're not still mad?"

I chuckle. "Not even close to mad, baby. I got over being mad the second you stood up and took your panties off for me. And that was before you gave me the best blowjob of my life." I brush her mussed hair out of her face. "Baby, I'm just sorry I lost my temper with you. And I'm sorry about that spanking—at least the first one. It wasn't for you, it was for me, and that's not cool."

She studies me, her eyes intelligent. I swear she sees right into my soul and doesn't judge. I don't know how that's possible. "I liked it."

I smile as my chest constricts. "I know you did. And I keep telling myself that makes it okay. But I'm not sure it does."

She covers my hand on her cheek with her palm. "Your concern makes it okay."

I shudder under her touch. "I don't know why you trust me so well, baby. I don't deserve it."

She purses her lips. "No, you don't."

I fight a smile, glad she's taking me to task. "Baby, I know I've been neglecting you and that's why you were trying to get a rise out of me. I called my younger brother and asked him to move here to help me run this shit so I can give you the attention you deserve. But please don't mess around with other guys because I will come unglued

167

and the asshole you touch will end up with his balls shoved up his ass. *Capiche?*"

She shivers slightly. "I'm sorry."

I already know she is, and I wasn't trying to make her say it again. I put my finger on her lips. "Listen, I'm going to make it up to you. I have to go back out there now, but I'm gonna clear my schedule for you tomorrow. I want you to pack a bag and be ready for me by 10 a.m. We're going to take a trip."

The flickering hope in her eyes scares the shit out of me. Not because I'm not going to do everything I fucking can to make sure I deliver whatever it is she needs from me, but because I want to be the man who delivers it permanently. And that's a fucking impossibility.

CHAPTER 12

 *ondra*

"Everyone's trying to figure out who you are," I murmur to Nico. We're sitting in the cafe of the Met, drinking espresso to revive ourselves from our long day of walking through the art museum. Yes, he flew me on a private jet to New York City this morning and demanded I show him all the best the Met had to offer. Considering it's my first trip to New York, let alone the Met, my bucket is beyond full.

Nico's as handsome as ever in one of his fine suits and he looks like some kind of celebrity amongst the tourists. He arches a brow. "Me? No, *amore*. They're looking at you. I heard one couple whispering that you're a famous actress." He picks up my hand and runs his thumb over my fingers.

If I'd worried that Nico and I would have nothing to

169

talk about if we actually had time to spend together, I was wrong. He told me all about growing up in Chicago—the things he misses from the city, the things he doesn't. How and why he ended up in Vegas.

I told him about Michigan, growing up across the street from Corey. How she became like a sister to me.

He rubs his stubbled jaw. "Here's the thing I keep wondering, Sondra."

"What?"

"How a woman as beautiful as you ended up in Reno with that lowlife bartender. It doesn't make sense. Why aren't you already married to some smart, nice intellectual who can talk about art and shit with you?"

I try to cover how much the question wounds me. Isn't it the same one I've asked myself three dozen times?

I draw in a breath. "Well. I guess I had a smart, nice intellectual for a boyfriend when I was getting my Masters. He cheated on me with my best friend. Tanner—"

"Don't say his name." Nico closes his eyes like I'm greatly testing his patience.

"—he wasn't the first to cheat on me. And John wasn't even the first. Before that, my boyfriend in high school hooked up with a girl while camped out in line for concert tickets to Coldplay."

Nico whistles. "That's a bad pattern."

"Yeah. I have terrible taste—" I break off too late. Nico's expression darkens.

I clear my throat. "Present company excluded, of course."

"No, you're right," he says. "I don't cheat. You don't

need to worry about that. But I'm all wrong for you. Definitely wrong."

The knife that's been in my chest since the day I met him twists and I lose my breath.

"Stop saying that." I should appreciate that he recognizes what a bad match we are, but I don't. I resent the hell out of it. Because every time feels like another rejection. It's just that this one isn't for another woman, it's for his job.

His life.

And I know he probably can't help it. He is who he is.

Nico sits taller, watching me intently. "Why, *cucciola mia?* We both know it's true."

My eyes fill with tears and I lunge up out of my chair. He catches my hand and pulls me to his lap, oblivious to everyone in the crowded cafe. His strong arms band around me. "I wish I could be someone else for you. I want to be. But I can't. I have family obligations you cannot fathom. I don't see how I'll ever be free of who and what I am."

I give up the struggle and collapse back against him. He's not saying he doesn't want me. I'm finally hearing the words for what they are. He's being realistic. Telling me he's a Tacone.

So the question is—can I live with all that means?

∼

Nico

. . .

WE GET BACK to the casino the next morning. I would've liked to stay longer, but until Stefano arrives, I can't leave the operation unmanned for long.

Sondra sucked my dick on the plane ride home, which made me feel like a fucking king.

I'm happy, maybe for the first time in my life. Not just satisfied. Not proud of some accomplishment, not drunk on power, but genuinely happy. Sondra's telling me all her plans for the casino redecoration, which is pure genius. She's figured out ways to use much of what's already in the Bellissimo, just rearranging it and categorizing things to fit into different Italian art movements and styles.

I escort her into the Bellissimo at the same time I hear Tony, who picked us up from the private airport, utter a low curse.

There, making a beeline straight for us, is a gorgeous leggy brunette.

Jenna Pachino.

"I'll handle this," Tony says. But I can't snub her. To do so could start a war. I'm in a tricky fucking situation and any wrong word could cause things to implode.

Cristo, Madonna e Dio, why didn't I deal with this situation sooner? Put more thought into the problem? Apply a little finesse? Now I'm about to fuck everything up.

"Jenna." I try to keep the stiffness out of my tone. I take her shoulders and we do the two-cheek kiss.

Sondra's gone rigid beside me.

Of course, this is her sore spot.

I put my hand on her back to reassure her, but Jenna's eyes track to it. Christ, I don't want her telling her dad I disrespected her.

I am so fucked.

Tony steps in to distract and they cheek-kiss.

"Tony, will you get Jenna anything she needs and take her up to my office?"

"Sure thing, boss."

"I'll be right up."

Jenna's gaze trails to Sondra. I haven't made the introduction. What in the fuck am I going to say? There's seriously nothing I can say that won't permanently fuck me over with one or both of them.

She doesn't look suspicious—more curious—but the undercurrent of tension is so thick between us, it's a wonder we can see through it.

Tony puts a hand on Jenna's lower back and escorts her away and I blow out my breath.

Sondra's turned pale, her expression flat.

"She's the daughter of another don in Chicago," I say as soon as she's out of earshot. "I don't know what she wants, but I have to meet with her. I will keep it brief."

Alarm flashes over Sondra's face and I know I've said the exact wrong thing.

For the life of me, though, I can't figure out how to dissipate this burgeoning disaster.

"Sondra?" I tuck a knuckle under her chin.

She jerks away.

"No." I make my voice firm. I have no idea why I chose to go hard with her, instead of coaxing, but it seems to work. She obeys the authority in my voice and turns back. I shake my head. "You think I'm fucking that girl, don't you?"

173

Her head wobbles on her neck. "Are you?" The tremor in her voice kills me.

"I've never touched her. *Ever.* Do you trust me?"

I hold my breath. Of course she doesn't fucking trust me. If she did, she wouldn't look like I just killed her kitten.

She shrugs. "I don't know, Nico. I have a bad history with this."

"*I know.*" I step into her space and grip her shoulders, showing how serious I am with the intensity of my gaze. "That's why I froze when she ambushed us. I didn't want you to get the wrong impression."

I see her waver. I'm making headway.

"Please trust me. I'm going to find out what she wants and get rid of her. I will not cheat on you. Ever. Can you believe that?"

Her lips tremble slightly, but she lifts her chin. "I want to. I just don't know."

I nod. That's probably as good as I'm going to get.

"I will prove it to you. Just give me a chance, okay, baby? I can't lose you now. I can't." I try to show her one small fraction of the vulnerability she offers me.

Her eyelashes flutter and she nods. I cup her face and kiss her—the most gentle kiss I've laid on her. It's as sweet as a promise. As sacred as a blessing.

She doesn't return it at first, but then she softens, moves her lips against mine. I stroke her hair. "Will you be in your suite?"

She nods.

"I'll find you there."

I kiss her again and leave.

Fuck. Now if only I can manage not to start a war over Jenna Pachino.

~

Jenna

MY MOTHER WANTED to come with me. My father wanted to send Alex as a bodyguard, but I refused. Being sent to visit my fiancé accompanied by the only man who's ever made my heart beat faster would make a difficult situation impossible.

I have a plan and after what I just saw down in the lobby, I think it just might work.

The trouble is, I don't know Nico Tacone at all. I've seen him at family parties, weddings and funerals, but I avoided him like the plague.

And he seemed to avoid me right back.

At least that's what I'm banking on.

So I sit in a plush chair outside his office with his pitbull Tony standing bodyguard at the door and try to get my heart out of my throat.

He doesn't make me wait long. Tacone arrives and holds the door open for me, the picture of gentlemanly manners.

I wipe my hands on my black jean skirt and enter.

"I heard you graduated," Tacone says politely. "Congratulations." He waves me into a chair across from his desk and takes a seat.

I swallow down the lump in my throat. "Thank you."

My hands tangle in my lap. My lips feel too dry. "My father says it's time for us to marry," I blurt.

Tacone's face remains blank, but I swear I see a muscle jump in his cheek.

"Are you—" I suck in a breath. "Are you prepared to marry me?"

Shoot. That was the wrong thing to say. Now I put him on the spot. He can't say no without offending my family.

He blinks at me. "Jenna—"

"Wait," I cut in. "I don't want to know the answer to that question. What I want to say, is…"

He's staring at me with polite brown eyes. There's really nothing wrong with this man. He seems quite nice. He's beyond rich. Definitely good-looking.

I should *want* to marry him. Especially considering how much it means to my father.

But I'm a bad daughter.

I want what I can't have—Alex.

"Would you consider releasing me from the contract?"

Tacone's brows shoot up to his hairline. "Yes." The word bursts out of him. Maybe I'm reading too much into it, but I imagine I hear the relief of twenty years of the same anxiety I've felt.

"I-I don't want to marry you. No offense."

His lips quirk. "None taken. Does your father know you're here?"

My shoulders sag. "Yes, but he sent me to pin you down on dates. He still wants us to go through with it."

Tacone drags a hand through his thick hair. "I haven't spoken to mine, either. I probably need to fly out and have a face to face with him. Make sure I can smooth it over. Giuseppe won't budge?"

I gnaw on my lip. "No, but maybe if he knew your family was canceling—"

Tacone sighs, defeat creeping into his expression. Yeah. We're right back to where we were as children, with our parents' contract firm, and our opinions inconsequential.

I suck in a breath, my heart hammering at what I'm about to say. "I could disappear for a while. I mean, I want to disappear. I'll send a letter saying I'm not going through with it. Send it to both our fathers and you. And then disappear. No one is to blame but me."

He rubs his jaw, his gaze astute. "Ah. And you're here running this plan by me because you need money to disappear?"

My stomach knots. I know mafia men. Better to come clean. Own it all. Put the cards on the table and let them decide what to do with you. "Yes. And I wanted to make sure you wouldn't be angry. I don't want to start a war."

He's quiet a long moment, simply regarding me. My father would be doing something with his hands— lighting a cigar or smoking it. Not Nico Tacone. It's hard not to squirm under his direct regard. Finally, he says, "Nor do I." He stands up and walks to a safe. "Yeah, I'll bankroll your disappearance. I got no problem with that. Bring me the letters first, and I'll set you up with whatever you need."

The sensation of wings taking flight in my chest is like nothing I've ever experienced. It's more than relief. It's freedom.

My life will be mine to live.

Mine, alone.

I dig in my purse and pull out three envelopes, already addressed and stamped but not sealed. I push them across the desk.

Tacone's lips quirk when he takes them and reads them one by one. They're identical, typed up but hand-signed.

"You need a new ID? Passport? Credit cards?"

I'm soaring. This is all too easy.

"Yes, please."

He nods and rises from the desk. "Okay. I'll have Tony set you up. He'll give you enough cash to get started, too. Whatever you need. But, Jenna?"

I look up at him. His expression goes stern. "Don't come back here. Don't contact me. You need something, you get in touch with Tony. He'll help you out. *Capiche*? And make sure he can get word to you, too. I'll let you know when the contract is dissolved."

I stand. I seriously want to kiss the guy's ring right now and swear my undying fealty. I just don't want to swear my life over to his marriage bed.

"Thank you, Mr. Tacone—Nico. Thanks for being so understanding and generous."

"Same." We give each other cheek-kisses and he opens the door and speaks in an undertone to Tony who nods and motions for me to come forward.

I step forward, into my future. My freedom.

The mafia princess sheds the crown.

 ondra

"GOOD MORNING, MS. SIMONSON," the security guy nods at me as I step out of the elevator. I get this preferential treatment all over the casino now. Word is out that I'm Nico's girl. I get waved to the front of the Starbuck's line, my favorite drink already prepared for me.

When I step out on the curb, the valet attendant already has Nico's Mercedes waiting for me. I take the keys and pretend driving a Mercedes is a totally normal thing for me.

It's hard not to eat it all up. It's hard not to let myself enjoy all that it means to be Nico Tacone's girlfriend.

But it's a total fantasy world. If I were going to stay here long-term, I'd need to get out and make friends, be in nature, build my own life.

For the moment, though, I'm letting myself enjoy it.

Nico stuffed a wad of cash in my purse this morning and told me to go clothes shopping. His cousin Sal is getting married this afternoon and we're invited. When I asked what to wear, he told me to buy a dozen outfits and let him pick.

Silly man. Silly, adorable, controlling man.

I've met Sal—he's one of the guys with a suite on the same floor as Nico—but we haven't talked. I know nothing about him. This will be the first time I get to engage with Nico's family, which I know he didn't want.

But if I'm really his girlfriend, and not some kept woman, I should bridge this gap. Figure out if I really could handle being permanently attached to a man born into a crime family.

Which probably means I should ask him some hard questions. How bloody are his hands? How legal is his business? Because from what I can tell, he's running a fully profitable casino. I'm not sure where the illegal part comes in.

But I'm sure it's there. And I don't know if I really want to know the answers.

I head to the Saks off 5th outlet and start pulling outfits. It's extravagant and ridiculous, and I never spend money on clothes for myself, but the fact that he gave me an assignment and wants to pick from the results makes it a fun game. I fill a cart with clothing and drag things into the dressing room, ten pieces at a time.

Two hours later, I'm laden with five giant bags of clothes, shoes and a jacket, and I head back to the casino. The valet attendant greets me like I'm the Princess of

Wales and the bellhop insists on carrying my shopping bags up to my room.

Nico enters a few minutes later without knocking.

"How'd you know I was back?"

His lips twitch. "I asked the valet to let me know."

I cock a hip. "I'm never sure whether to be flattered or creeped out by how controlling you are."

Nico shoves his hands in his pockets. It's a signal of harmlessness—he's not advancing on me for once. "I know I talk a lot of shit, baby. I like to pretend I own you. But I would never stop you from doing anything you wanted to do, even if it meant walk out of here and never come back." The words seem to cost him, because the muscles in his throat tighten and a muscle ticks in his jaw.

I close the distance between us, press my body up against his. His strong arms band around me. "That's all I need to know," I murmur.

"Sondra," he murmurs, leaning his forehead against mine. "You're one in a million. The way you always take me for what I am."

I swallow. Now is the time for the difficult conversation. "Nico...tell me the worst. Who are you? What are you involved in? What have you done?"

His arms tighten around me and his face goes pale. "Do I need to search you for a wire?" The joke is forced and neither of us smile.

"Truly, Sondra, I can't tell you. I wouldn't tell you anything that would put you in an awkward or dangerous position—with my family or the feds. And don't think I don't know you have an uncle in the FBI."

I flush and shove his chest. "You still think I'm a spy?"

181

"Of course I don't. No, no, no. Listen." He cradles my face. "What prompted this? Why are you asking?" I look away, but he turns my face back. "Are you trying to figure out if you can stay?"

I nod.

He blows out a long, slow exhale. "I'll tell you this. I left Chicago because I didn't want blood on my hands. I didn't want to spend my life looking over my shoulder for the next gunman or Fed trying to bring me down. I believed big corporations do the same kind of shit my family did on the street, on a large scale and it's legal. And I wanted that. Large scale, legal business. I already knew about gambling, so I came to Vegas.

"But I was bankrolled by the family, which means I can't ever be truly free. I launder their money. I still employ the old-school tactics of intimidation and fear when necessary. Not murder," he shakes his head. "No drugs. No sex trade. Nothing else illegal. And if I could cut ties and go one hundred percent legit today, I'd do it. I just haven't figured out how." He strokes my face with his thumb. "So now you know. That's everything. Well, almost everything. I have one death on my hands from when I got *made*. It's a requirement. It made me sick and it solidified my resolve to get out and never go back." There's a wobble in his voice and I throw myself against him, pressing my cheek against his chest.

I want to tell him I'm sorry for his family, his past, but how do I say that without negating who he is now? So I just hold him, show him I'm still here. Still on his side. Whatever side that is.

~

Nico

IT WAS SHORT NOTICE, but Sal managed to book a decent private chapel—not the cheesy Elvis kind on the strip. I pull into the chapel parking lot and turn off the Porsche I took out for the drive today. We get out and I escort Sondra toward the door. She's wearing a pair of tight white capri jeans with pink-gold heels and a turquoise blouse. She looks classy and beautiful.

Sal's marrying a stripper he hired a year ago. He's been banging her ever since and decided last week, when she told him she was pregnant, to make it official. He swore me to secrecy over her former profession, which I have no problem with. I actually like the girl. She's a Jersey chick, street smart but generous. She'll fit in with the family, make a good mother to his kids.

I can't tell if I've won or lost something with Sondra. It appears to be a win, but she's quiet on the ride to the chapel. She went soft, which is always her gift to me, but who knows what conclusions she'll draw from what I told her. What decisions she'll make.

I'll honor them, whatever they are. Even if it kills me to let her go.

"Nico!" My aunt calls from the parking lot.

I stop and wait for her and two other cousins to arrive. My uncle, her husband, is in jail for life, which is why I took Sal under my wing when I moved here. She and the girls flew out on my plane this morning. "Aunt Perla, this

RENEE ROSE

is Sondra. Sondra, this is Sal's mother, my Aunt Perla, and his little sisters, Genevieve and Kara."

Leo pulls up and then Sal arrives in his own car, appearing harried and on edge. "Where's the bride?" I call out.

His head whips around as he scans the parking lot, panic flaring in his eyes until his gaze lands on a red mustang parked up front. "She's here. She and her girl-friends came early."

He hugs his mother and sisters, pumps my hand, cheek-kisses Sondra and slaps Leo on the back.

"Sal, this is not a Catholic church," his mother complains. "I can't believe you're getting married in a non-denominational chapel."

"I know, Ma. This was the best I could get on short notice."

Aunt Perla sniffs and I hold the door open. The whole lot troops in and we walk through an indoor area to a back courtyard with a set of fake boulders and a waterfall cascading down the center.

"This is pretty," Sondra murmurs politely.

I think the shape of the rocks kinda looks like butt cheeks, but I keep my mouth shut.

The officiant directs us to take a seat on the plastic folding chairs, dressed up with fabric skirts and canned organ music starts to play. The bride comes in with her two bridesmaids—also strippers, I suspect—and they meet Sal up at the butt cheek waterfall.

Thank fuck the officiant keeps it short and sweet. I hold Sondra's hand during the ceremony and Aunt Perla even finds the grace to cry a bit.

"And now I'd like to invite you all to a celebration dinner at Scordetto's Italian Restaurant," I announce.

"Is that a restaurant at your casino, Nico?" Aunt Perla asks.

I shake my head. "No, Sal doesn't want to celebrate his wedding at the place he works. I rented out a nice restaurant for the night. Come on, let's go."

"That was sweet of you," Sondra murmurs as I lead her out.

"Least I could do." I open her car door and help her in. The truth is, I'm already getting itchy about mixing family with Sondra. Later I would think it was my gut warning me, but all I think now is how uneducated and unrefined they must seem to her. It's shitty of me to be ashamed of my roots, but I guess I've pulled myself up pretty far from where I came from. I forget how far until moments like these.

~

Sondra

NICO SEEMS DISTRACTED and uncomfortable when we get to the restaurant, and I totally sympathize. Who doesn't get squirmy around family gatherings?

I head to the women's room and when I come out of the stall, I hear Nico's aunt and Sal talking in the hallway outside.

"So what's the story with Nico's girlfriend?"

I freeze, my hand on the door to push it open.

"Yeah, she's nice. Makes him happy," Sal answers.

"Yeah, but what about the fiancée? Isn't he still engaged to Jenna Pachino?"

Jenna Pachino. I knew it!

I go ice cold and hot at the same time. My stomach drops to my feet on the floor.

Oh my fucking God. I knew his story didn't add up. The way he didn't introduce me when she showed up at the casino. She's his fucking *fiancée*?

This is my pattern. Cheating assholes. Even when I know they're lying, I still want to believe. And this time? This time I don't think I'm ever going to recover.

I back away from the door, shaking like someone who's gone into shock.

Oh yeah. I have gone into shock. Somehow I manage to pull out my phone. "Corey?" Fuck, I'm already crying.

My cousin must hear everything in my voice. "What's wrong?"

"I need you to pick me up—from Scordetto's. Please come soon."

"I'll be right there. Are you safe? Hurt?"

"I'm okay, I just need to get out of here right away."

I hear a door slam. "I'm already on my way," she promises.

I wait with my ear pressed to the door until I'm sure no one's outside before I slip out. The group is gathered in the back room, ordering drinks, so I'm able to get out the front door without anyone seeing me. I skulk around the side of the building like a criminal and wait. It feels like hours, but probably isn't more than ten minutes before Corey's car comes screeching into the parking lot.

I run for it, just as Nico comes out.

"Sondra!" he shouts as I throw open the car door. "Wait! Where are you going?" He jogs toward the car.

"Get out of here!" I sob to Corey.

She steps on the gas, but Nico throws himself in front of the car, forcing Corey to slam on the brakes.

"Sondra! What happened?" He runs around to my side of the car.

"Where's your fiancée, Nico? Why didn't you bring her today?"

If I had any doubt in my mind the fiancée was real, it evaporates when I see Nico go still.

"Drive away," I tell Corey.

"Wait!" Nico lunges for the car as Corey guns it. "Let me explain."

I flip him the bird and we peel out of the driveway.

And then I'm a sobbing mess. "I picked another cheater. Can you believe it? I really can't."

Corey throws me a worried glance. "I'm so sorry, Sondra. He deserves to die."

"Well, I wouldn't go that far," I say, smearing tears across my cheek with the back of my hand.

My phone dings with a text coming in. I know it's from Nico, but I'm too stupid not to look.

I'm not marrying Jenna. I barely even know her. It was a contract made by our fathers when we were kids. She came here to ask me to help release it, which I'm doing. I never intended to marry her. I only want to be with you.

I read it aloud to Corey, who presses her lips together. "Well, he should've told you about it, then."

My sobs quiet. I think I actually believe him, which

187

might be total insanity. "Yes, he should have." It doesn't matter, though. All I know is that I can't trust my own judgment with this guy.

I block his number on my phone.

"Where to?" Corey asks.

"Home."

"My place?"

"No. Michigan. I want to go home. Take me to the airport."

CHAPTER 14

I'M GOING out of my mind.

I can't get her fucking cousin to talk—to tell me where she is. At least not with any non-violent methods of persuasion, and obviously I'm not going to strong-arm her. I have a guy watch Corey's house, but she doesn't seem to be there. Nor has she appeared on any camera in the casino.

My girl is gone.

Even though this whole time I knew I was wrong for her, I can't stand knowing I hurt her. I pressed a knife right into her soft spot and let her feel cheated on again.

It's unforgivable.

And that's the part I have to make right. I can't let her walk away from this thing wounded. I never wanted that. I was selfish—I indulged in getting close to her. I let myself get carried away by the pleasure she brought to me. But once I convince her I was true, I need to let her go.

It's the only way I can make any of this right.

Sondra

I'M in bed with the covers over my head for the third day in a row. My mom has been in a dozen times to coax me out, but I'm not having it.

"Just let me rest," I tell her. "I need sleep."

My phone rings and I ignore it. A text comes through. I ignore that. It rings again.

I look at the screen.

Corey.

I pick up. "Hey." Even to my own ears, my voice sounds heavier than lead.

"I think Nico's story is true," Corey says.

My stomach, nervous and empty on the depression diet of a few bites of fruit and toast, seizes up.

"He's talked to me. I cornered his cousin Sal, and I even asked that guy Leo and his bodyguard Tony. They all had the same story. Childhood commitment that's never been acted on. In fact, Tony says he gave her money to disappear while Nico gets things worked out with her dad." Her voice lowers. "He also says Nico's a total wreck. Hasn't slept since you left."

"Why are you telling me this?" If there's panic in my

voice, it's because I spent the last three days reconciling myself to never seeing Nico again. Now Corey's shoving open the door I've been trying so hard to keep closed.

"I just thought you should know. He still should have told you about the fiancée situation, but with your past, maybe you jumped to the worst conclusion. He wasn't two-timing you, Sondra."

I throw back the covers, suddenly too antsy to be in bed. "It doesn't matter. It's not like I was going to marry him, anyway. An ending would've been inevitable. So now it's done." I pad to the bathroom, the need for a shower overwhelming.

"I don't know. I think you were thinking about whether you could be with him long term. And that's sort of a different question. I'm not sure you should mix up the two situations."

"Are you seriously on his side now?" I snap.

"No! I'm totally on your side. I support you no matter what you decide. But I don't think you should choose based on whatever feelings came up because you thought he was cheating. I'm pretty sure he wasn't."

I stand still in the bathroom, the phone pressed too hard against my ear. "Okay. Thanks."

"You okay?"

"No. But I will be." I hang up and take a long shower. It's time to come back to the world of the living.

I have some decisions to make.

CHAPTER 15

ico

MY PRIVATE INVESTIGATOR found a plane ticket in Sondra's name to Michigan on the night of the wedding. I rent a car in Detroit and drive an hour and a half to Marshall. I'm wearing a pair of jeans and a short-sleeved button down. It's my attempt at removing the mafia from my appearance. Figuring out how to at least get through Sondra's parents' front door.

I've been shot at. Had the crap beat out of me. Made million dollar deals. Nothing's made me sweat like this.

I figure I have only one shot at this, and I don't know if I can pull it off. When I get to Marshall, I stop to buy flowers, but then I decide they're too cliché. Sondra doesn't need flowers or money from me. She needs... I don't know what she needs, but I suspect it's somehow baring my soul.

193

Which I'm willing to do.

I show up at her parents' house and ring the bell. A pretty woman in her mid-fifties answers the door. She wears an expectant smile, which fades as she takes in my face. "You must be Nico," she says. There's disappointment and judgment in her voice. I definitely have my work cut out for me.

"Yes, ma'am."

A man who must be Sondra's father appears behind her.

Well, it's time to eat humble pie. "I know I hurt your daughter, but I'm here to make it right. I'd just like a chance to talk to her."

"She's not here," her mother says.

My chest tightens. Am I going to call bullshit? I know she came to Marshall. "Where—"

"She went on a walk." Her mother lifts her chin toward the sidewalk behind me.

"Oh." Relief pours through me. Every cell in my body wants to bolt out to that sidewalk and follow it all over town until I find her. But I haven't even won the battle with her parents yet.

"May I come in?"

Apparently they're too much the nice Midwesterners to refuse me entry. Her mother opens the screen and both of them back away from the door. I step into their sweet, middle-class home and have a seat when her father waves me to the sofa. He clears his throat and offers me something to drink, which I refuse.

"I want you both to know I'm serious about your daughter. Of course, I'll honor her decision, but I love her and I want to spend the rest of my life with her. Have a family, even." My voice chokes a little and I clear it. "I'll take good care of her. And I'll support her career one hundred percent. She's a smart, talented woman and I know she'll succeed at anything she tries."

The tension has gone out of her parents. I don't know if I've won them over, but I've at least softened them. It's a start.

"Well, I don't really know what happened between you two, but Sondra's been heartbrok—"

"Mom."

I surge to my feet at the sound of Sondra's voice. She's standing outside the screen door. I forget to wait for an invite as I stalk around to the front door and throw it open. "Sondra."

She's pale. Dark circles under her eyes mar her beautiful face. "What's going on?" she demands. She gives me an up and down sweep of her eyes. "And what are you wearing?"

"I'm trying to fit in," I murmur and step out of the house. "May I walk with you? Or would you like to take a drive?" My brain revs up, trying to come up with something more appealing to offer, but she says, "Yeah, okay."

Relief nearly drops me to my knees. "Walk or drive?"

She looks at the rental car—the Ford Explorer was the best I could get—and raises her eyebrows. "Let's walk."

"Okay." I take her hand, not sure if she's going to shake me off, but she lets me. Hers is clammy and cold. "Sondra, I never fucked around on you or any other woman. You need to know that."

"I know."

My step falters. She sounds so quiet, so certain. "You do?"

"Yeah. Corey talked to Tony and Sal and Leo. They all said the same thing you did."

"I should've told you about the problem. To be honest, I spent my whole life keeping it under the rug where I didn't have to think about it. A dilemma for tomorrow— know what I mean?"

She looks up at me and I swear I see sympathy in the softness of her eyes. I draw a breath and barrel forward. "Jenna Pachino came to Vegas because her father sent her to force my hand, but she wants no part of this arranged marriage. We agreed she should run away for a while until I get things resolved. I gave her money to disappear. That's all that's between us, I swear to *La Madonna*. That's the most we've ever talked. The only time we've been alone in a room together. Before that, we avoided each other like the plague."

"I don't want to talk about her anymore, Nico."

My heart stops. Restarts unevenly. I halt and turn her to face me, hold her other hand like we're a bride and groom at the altar. "Do you want to talk about us?"

She nods. "I heard what you told my parents." Her voice is choked.

My throat closes. "I want to marry you, *amore*. I want to figure out how to make this work. And it's fucking complicated. Would you—" I draw a breath. "Would you want me if I had nothing? No casino, no family?"

Surprise flares in her eyes. She licks her lips. "You could create it all again. You could create anything."

Now I'm surprised. I expected resistance, major convincing. She's going easy on me.

"Does that mean—are you considering? Are you willing?"

～

Sondra

I DIDN'T KNOW how badly I'd want Nico to hold me. To promise the moon and the sun or maybe just to take charge and carry me off. Tell me I'm his and he's tying me to the bed until I swear it.

But I have to be strong right now. I have to be a big girl and choose for me.

"I don't know," I whisper.

Nico drops to his knees, right there on the sidewalk. Tears blur my vision. "I need you, Sondra. I didn't have a purpose to living before I met you. You brought light where there was only darkness. You give to me—receive me with no walls up. I don't know how you do it, but I can't live without you."

"Get up, Nico," I mumble between trembling lips. I try to tug him back to his feet. Tears track down my cheeks.

"I don't even know what I can offer you, but I promise it will be everything I have. Everything."

"Yes. *Yes.* Nico, I want you."

He falls back and drags me down to his lap. People driving by are looking at us like we're lunatics and I totally don't give a crap. "You want me?" His voice is torn, broken.

I hold his face between my hands. "Yes. I do."

The hardness returns to his face, but it's not frightening, it's thrilling. Because it's steely determination and force. The same force that makes me quiver every time he sets his sights on me.

"Marry me?"

"Yes."

He gathers me and pulls us both up to our feet. "Good." He holds my hand and starts pulling me toward my house. His shoulders are squared, his walk brisk, like he's heading to battle. "There's just one major wrinkle to iron out. After that, I'm sure we'll figure out the rest together. Okay, baby?"

"Yes. Okay."

We arrive in front of my house and he goes straight for the car. "I have a bag of your things already—from the casino. Go say goodbye to your parents. Tell them we're going to buy a ring and we'll be in touch with a wedding date."

He winks at me and leans against the vehicle.

I don't mind seeing him restored to his cocky, bossy self. In fact, I rather love it, as much as I treasure knowing he humbled himself before me.

Nico Tacone, the powerful man who needs me.

Sondra

. . .

NICO'S quiet on the drive and he won't say where we're going. At first I think we're driving to Chicago, until we eventually pull up at a Federal Correctional Institute in Pekin, Illinois, and I realize we're visiting his dear old dad.

Nico turns to face me in the vehicle after we park. "I swear to *Cristo*, I will never ask this of you again. But I want him to meet you. I'm gonna try to get his blessing for our union."

Nerves flutter in my belly, but I nod.

He nods back and we get out. "I'm on the approved visitor list. I have a contact who should be greased enough to let us both through." We walk up to the check-in area and I watch Nico make eye contact with a guy who comes hustling forward. There's a brief interchange, and suddenly we're at the front of the line, being searched for weapons and escorted into the visiting area.

Don Santo Tacone comes in wearing his orange prison uniform. He's an older version of Nico, but without any of the life in his eyes. They are cold, flinty orbs and when they flick over me, the cold shiver of death runs down my spine.

Nico produces a couple of paperback books—already checked by the guards—and pushes them under the glass divider.

His father doesn't even look at them. Instead he stares at me. Hard. "Who's she?"

"My fiancée."

His brows flick. "The hell she is."

"I'm not asking."

My stomach twists in a knot. I'm sweaty and cold, scared for Nico. Scared for us.

His father's eyes narrow and he shifts his focus to Nico. "You would choose her over family?"

Nico blinks rapidly, then nods.

Don Santo directs his attention to me, looking me up and down again critically. "Why?"

Nico swallows. "She's...the missing piece to me. I need her."

"You don't make decisions that affect this whole family. Only I make those. You are nothing without us," he spits.

Nico's never looked more sober. "Perhaps not. But I'd still have her."

His father gets up and walks out.

I want to puke. I don't know what Nico expected from this meeting, but I somehow don't think it went according to plan.

We get up and leave. Nico doesn't speak until we're in the vehicle.

"So, now what?" I ask, my voice shaky.

Nico doesn't look at me. His face is a hard mask as he starts the car, staring straight ahead. "So now either everything's fine or there will be trouble."

I choke on my own spit. "What kind of trouble?"

He reaches for my hand and gives it a squeeze. "Nothing will happen to you. This is just between family."

"Nico. H-how long until things are settled?"

"Oh, very soon. I'd give it no more than forty-eight hours." He takes the exit toward Chicago. "So we'll let things cook. The resolution will come out soon. In the meantime, I'm going to buy you the biggest fucking diamond in the Windy City."

"I don't need a diamond," I murmur, fear squeezing my heart.

I'm not sorry I chose Nico. Not after what I just saw. He's willing to alienate himself from his entire family for me. But I'm definitely scared. Totally out of my element.

"You're getting a diamond." Nico's mood seems to lighten. "You're going to let me spoil you this time."

His love seems to wrap around me and squeeze. "Okay," I murmur. Whatever makes him happy.

WE END up finding a pear-shaped diamond at Tiffany's. When we get back to the Explorer, three guys are leaning up against it, arms folded in full tough guy stances. Nico goes rigid, but his step only falters for a second.

"Give me the keys," one of them orders. He resembles Nico, but older.

Nico tosses him the keys.

His brother—I'm assuming it's his brother—hits the fob to unlock the doors and the two other guys throw open the doors. "Get in."

Nico helps me in the backseat and slides in beside me.

"Put her on your lap," one of the guys growls as they sandwich us in the backseat. One of them has a gun pointed at us.

His brother searches the glove box and under the seat. "You didn't bring a piece?" There's a mocking tone to his voice, like Nico got caught with his pants down.

"I didn't," Nico confirms.

His brother looks in the rearview mirror. "What the fuck are you wearing?"

Nico doesn't respond. His brother drives the car and when we head out of the city, one of the guys produces two blindfolds, which he ties around our heads. I was moderately freaked out before. Now I'm ready to piss myself.

The Explorer slows down and pulls off on what must be a dirt road. I hear another vehicle following behind us. Nico's arms band tightly around my waist, as if by holding onto me, he'll be able to protect me from whatever's about to happen.

We stop. The car behind us pulls in, too. My blindfold gets pulled off, but Nico's doesn't.

A fourth guy comes out from behind the wheel of a black Range Rover. The doors fly open and they drag us out. His brother restrains me. One of the other guys produces rope and ties Nico's wrists behind his back, then they force him to his knees.

And then they take turns punching him in the face.

"Nico!" I scream, struggling against his brother's hold.

Nico attempts to lunge to his feet. "Junior, you touch one hair on her head—"

"I'm not hurting her." Junior almost sounds amused. "I'm just restraining her."

It's true. His hands are huge, like Nico's, but he hasn't grabbed with bruising force. He wrapped my arms around my waist to restrain me, holding me with little effort.

Nico calms slightly.

"This is the girl you're willing to give up everything

for?" his brother asks. One of the thugs punches Nico in the face again and drops of blood fly from his mouth.

I scream.

"Yeah."

"Everything? You think she'll still want you when you're poor?"

"I want him, just let him go—" I thrash my legs around, trying to pull free.

"You can't have her if you're dead." All amusement leaves his voice—the cold threat hangs menacingly still in the air.

"No," I scream. "Don't kill him. I'll leave him alone. I'll go away. Please...I'm sorry. Let him go. I won't interfere."

Nico doesn't move. He stands on his knees, head held high, unmoving, even when the thugs punch him in the ribs.

"Hmm? You'd rather be dead than live without her?"

Nico spits blood from his lips. The lower one is split. He nods. "Yeah."

"Noooo," I scream. It echoes through the trees. My throat rasps.

This is all my fault. He did this for me. I had no idea what it would cost him. What he'd be risking.

Junior cocks his gun and holds it to my head. "What if I kill her, too?"

Nico's face contorts beneath the blindfold, rage twisting his features. I've never seen him look so horrifying. He attempts to lunge to his feet. The two soldiers grab his shoulders and push him back down, laying punches into his unprotected gut.

"I will fucking destroy everything you've ever loved,"

Nico snarls.

Junior gives a mirthless chuckle. "That would be hard to do from the grave."

"Believe it," Nico spits.

Junior releases his hold on me. "I believe it." He lifts his chin at the goons, who abruptly step back from Nico. Junior walks forward and pulls a knife from his belt.

"No, please!" I rush forward and lunge for Junior's arm, but one of the soldiers catches me around the waist first.

"Easy with her," Junior warns.

Easy with me? My brain scrambles to understand why, but then Junior reaches past Nico and uses the blade to cut the rope tying his hands.

"Where's Jenna Pachino?" Junior asks.

"I gave her money to disappear for a while. Tony's gonna let her know when things are settled."

"They're settled. I talked to Old Man Pachino. We have a new alliance. You're off the fucking hook."

Junior grasps Nico's face with both hands, and lifts him to his feet. He yanks off the blindfold and kisses his brother on each cheek. Then he turns and stalks back toward their Range Rover. I think I hear him mutter, "Welcome to the family," as I run past him to Nico.

Nico spreads his arms and catches me in them.

I weep, squeezing him for all I'm worth.

"Easy, baby. Not so tight."

Oh Christ. I yank away. He probably has cracked ribs. Bruised, for sure.

The car doors shut—all four men have climbed inside the Range Rover, leaving us alone.

"It's all right, come here." He pulls me against him, kissing the top of my head. "Are you hurt?"

"*Me?*" I squeak.

"Are you?" His voice sharpens, like there will be hell to pay if I am.

"No, not at all." I draw a shuddering breath against him, my tears moistening his blood splattered shirt.

His large body relaxes. He rubs my back and strokes my hair. "Everything's going to be okay."

"It is? What's happening?"

"It was a test. Or maybe a reckoning. A little of both, I guess."

I tip my head up, blinking my wet lashes to see his bruised face. "A test? Did you know that?"

He shrugs. "I was about sixty percent sure."

Sixty percent sure he wouldn't die for me.

My knees wobble and I lean into him. "So you passed?"

Nico laughs through bloody lips. "Yeah, baby. Everything's fine. We're going to get married. You're going to redecorate the Bellissimo. My little brother Stefano's gonna help me run the casino and I'm gonna focus my hours on making you happy."

I nuzzle my face into his chest. "I already am happy," I murmur.

And it's true. I'm definitely shaken up by what just happened, but rather than changing my mind about binding my life to Nico's, his utter and complete commitment to me solidified it. I understand he's part of a world that isn't pretty, but he'd do anything for me. Even give up his life.

So I have faith we will figure out the rest.

EPILOGUE

 lex

I ACCEPT another glass of champagne and down it in a single gulp. From my position against the center pillar, I have a view of the entire reception.

I'm surprised the Tacones went all out on Nico's wedding, considering what it means to the Pachino family. I guess Junior Tacone worked something out with Don Guiseppe, but it seems like a slap in the face, if you ask me.

Of course, no one asked me.

The wedding is at one of the finest hotels in Chicago—top floor, wall-to-wall windows overlooking the city and Lake Michigan. The bride is sweet—not the type I'd ever guess Nico would go for, but pretty, if you're into that wholesome blonde kinda thing. Her family came from Michigan—a bunch of nerdy small-town WASPs, with the exception of her maid of honor, a leggy redhead who looks like she could hold her own with any of ours. And, if I'm reading the body language right, she might already be entangled with Nico's younger brother Stefano.

Nico dances with his mom, his bride with her father. It's so sweet it makes my teeth hurt.

Of course I heard Nico got a beatdown for wanting out of the contract, even though Jenna's the one who ran away. I also heard Nico might have bankrolled that disappearance. I've been fucking waiting for permission to verify that fact.

Because every goddamn day that girl is missing has me itching to punch another hole in my wall. I can't stand not knowing if she's safe or in trouble. If she needs my help.

The fact that she went to Tacone for help in the first place kills me, but I guess it makes sense. She needed him to kill the marriage contract. I guess for that reason, I should be grateful to Tacone.

But I'm not.

I want to kill the bastard for knowing something about Jenna Pachino I don't.

Don G walks over and offers me a cigar. I accept, even though I don't really enjoy them. It makes the old man happy, and that's part of my job.

"It's time," he rasps.

I don't recall being given a job. "For what?"

"To bring my daughter back."

My heart picks up speed.

"The Tacone boy knows where she is. Find out. Go to her. Straighten her out. Bring her home to me. She's played the disobedient daughter long enough."

Thank fuck.

I push away from the pillar. "I'll make sure it's done."

"I know you will. That's why I asked you."

I dart a glance at him. Jenna Pachino's been off-limits for my entire life. Well, *her* entire life, since I'm six years older. The point is, I've never been allowed to look at the girl, much less indulge in the kind of fantasies I want her to play a starring role in.

So when Don G says he asked me, in particular, for this job, I can't tell if he's putting me on notice to watch my ass and keep my hands off her, or if he's giving me permission to court her.

I know one thing: when I find Jenna Pachino, I'm going to take my time with the *straighten her out* directive before I bring her home.

Because in my mind, Jenna Pachino has always belonged to me.

The End

GRAB YOUR BONUS material from King of Diamonds here.

I hope you enjoyed *King of Diamonds*. If you loved it, please consider reviewing it or recommending to a friend —your reviews help indie authors so much.

Want more *Vegas Underground*? Read Stefano and Corey's book, ***Jack of Spades***, Jenna and Alex's short story, ***Mafia Daddy***, Tony and Pepper's book ***Ace of Hearts*** and

Junior's book *Joker's Wild,* and Alessia and Vlad's book *His Queen of Clubs.*

You may also enjoy my first mafia series, *The Bossman* (read on for the sample chapter).

—SIGN **up for my mailing list**: http://owned.gr8.com.

--**Get text alerts of my new releases** by Texting: EZLXP55001 to 474747

--**Join Renee's Romper Room**, my Facebook reader group by **emailing me** with the email you use for Facebook. It's a secret group (because we discuss kink) so I have to send you an invite to join.

WANT MORE? JACK OF SPADES EXCERPT

Chapter One - Jack of Spades

Corey

Three kinds of gamblers spend big at my roulette table.

There's the guy who's all up in his head. He's quiet, body language closed. He sits with hunched shoulders and barely meets my eye. He plays odds, usually has a system he sticks to religiously. Like he always plays red and doubles his bet when he loses.

Then there's the reckless gambler. He's riding emotion, drugs or alcohol. He's the opposite of the first kind. No system, totally haphazard. He might ask the woman beside him for her favorite number and bet it.

Then, there's the gut gambler, my personal favorite. He carries an electricity with him that often carries the entire table away. It's the guy who's found the magic. Lady Luck, mojo, their stars aligning—who knows what it is, but they have an energy they're following. They stay in the flow, following their intuition and bet right every time.

Often they appear similar to reckless gamblers: they're outgoing, social. They engage with the people around them, including me, their croupier.

The whale—that's Vegas for big spender—at my table tonight is neither reckless, nor a gut gambler, although he has the personality and style of both. He's gorgeous with a finely tailored suit and European flair, like he stepped off the pages of an Italian men's magazine. He flirts shamelessly with me and chats up the people around him.

I scoop and stack the chips and award the winnings with practiced finesse, doing a one-handed split and stack and moving with lightning speed.

"There she goes, beauty and talent."

It's cheesy, but I flash him a smile. I like having him at my table, love his charm and flair, the big tips, yet my spidey sense keeps sounding. There's something off about him.

He's down two thousand at the moment. He slides his chips out onto the table at the last minute, right as I wave my hand and call no more bets. He sets them up sloppily, too. I can't tell if he wants them in the box for *Third Twelve* or *Odd*.

"Which one, sir?" I lean forward to get his attention as the wheel spins.

He's been drinking quite a bit, but he doesn't appear intoxicated. His eyes flick to my cleavage—which I still manage to work despite the masculine uniform—then back to my face before he gives me a slow, good-natured grin. "Odds, please. Sorry for that."

"No slop," I warn, and scoot the chips over as the ball settles.

He wins. He slides two hundred-dollar chips across the table to me as a tip. When I pull his chips in, I see he's embedded a ten dollar chip in the middle instead of a hundred. I flick my gaze up and see he's watching me. He winks.

Asshole.

I subtly signal for Security to come over.

It's not the first time I've been propositioned to cheat for a customer. It happens often enough. It sort of boggles my mind that he'd spend two hundred bucks paying me off to make ninety. But I suppose it was a test. Once he found out if I'd give him anything, he would've tried it again and again.

Vincent, the security manager on the floor tonight ambles over and stands close to me, dipping his head to listen.

"This guy's playing slop and trying to slip low chips in his stack."

Later, I would realize Vincent seemed a little too pleased with me, but it doesn't register. I'm just ignoring the flutters in my belly as he walks around to escort the dude out. I'm not sorry. I did the right thing, for sure. I'm only disappointed because the guy was attractive and sort of fascinating to me, and I'd fantasized for just a moment about him asking me out.

But whatever. I'm not going to risk this job, not even for a sexy man in a sharp suit. Working at the Bellissimo is like a job, education and socialization all rolled into one glamorous package. It's owned by the notorious Nico

Tacone, of the Tacone Chicago crime family, who rules the place with an iron fist. I wouldn't fuck with him. Even if he is in love with my cousin.

I finish my shift and head toward the employee locker rooms. When I pass the hallway toward the security offices, I stop short.

Vincent is standing in a relaxed posture, shooting the shit with none other than the sexy suit from my table.

"Corey," he grins and beckons me closer. "Come here, I want to introduce you to someone."

Oh Jesus. He was a secret shopper. Or whatever you call a security test. I don't know why it pisses me off, but it does. My stomach tightens up into a knot as I stride over.

"Corey, meet Stefano Tacone, our new Head of Security."

I lift my hand to slap Stefano's face. I don't know why I do it. Yes, I have a redhead's temper and I grew up in a violent family. Still, I should know better.

He catches my wrist and uses it to pull me right up against him. "I wouldn't." His warning is less a growl than a low, smoky rumble. Like he's dirty-talking me right here in the hallway.

My body responds immediately, my core turning molten. Of course, my damn cheeks heat, too. And believe me, on a redhead, there's no mistaking a blush.

"No one strikes a Tacone without regretting it." It's a threat, yet it's still spoken good-naturedly, with the same heart-stopping charm he used out on the floor, trying to get me to cheat for him.

Shit. Did I actually just lift a hand to a mob boss? A chill slithers down my back.

I'm so going to lose my job.

Except Stefano doesn't look angry. He looks like he wants to eat me for lunch.

I figure my best bet is to own my mistake. "Forgive me."

Stefano

The beauty in my arms—well, not quite in my arms, more at my mercy—meets my gaze with courage.

I see neither fear nor defiance in the bright blue eyes, merely bald curiosity, almost a hint of fascination.

Likewise, bella.

I picked her table for a reason, and it wasn't because anyone suspected her of cheating. Quite the opposite. The floor manager says she always attracts a crowd of gentlemen, earns big tips. She's fast and showy, exuding just the right balance of cool professional and warm invitation in any game she deals. I tested her because we need a dealer for private games upstairs.

Now, though, I want to play all kinds of private games with her and none of them involve a deck of cards or a roulette wheel.

"I don't like being humiliated," she says. For a moment, I think she's speaking to my thoughts, and then I realize it's her justification for trying to slap me. She turns her wrist in my hand, attempting to get free.

I don't allow it, pulling her small hand up to my mouth to brush my lips across her knuckles. "I'll remember that," I murmur.

She goes still, throat working on a swallow. She's so close I sense the heat of her lanky body, notice the slight tremble in her fingers, despite the evenness of her gaze.

There goes the blush again, giving her away. I want to keep holding her tight against my body, watching those electric blue eyes dilate every time I speak, but if I do, I'll end up shoving her against the wall and having my way with the tits she wields like weapons.

No other female croupier looks like this one. The new uniform is a white oxford, crimson vest, and a bow tie, for God's sake.

Corey manages to make the outfit sinful, though. The short black skirt hugs every curve of her ass, hips and waist, setting off a pair of long slender legs. She has the blouse unbuttoned and open to the vest, the bow tie worn on the inside like a lover's collar. How I'd love to put a collar and leash on this beautiful creature and bring her to heel; she'd take some training, too. The *coupe de grace* of the outfit is her vest. She chose one two sizes too small, making it appear more like a bustier or corset, cinching below her breasts and pushing them in and up until they're begging to spill from her blouse. I can't tell with the vest if her nipples are hard, but judging from her parted lips and short breath, I'd guess they are.

I know I sprouted a chub just from getting rough with her. Which would probably be a good reason to let her go. I force a little self-control and release her.

"Come into my office, let's have a little chat." I wave my arm to indicate my new office.

Again, she holds her head high, tossing her long thick waves over her shoulder as she precedes me to the closed door.

She waits for me to open it, presumably because it's my office, but I take distinct satisfaction in reaching past her to hold it open, like we're on some kind of classy date instead of interview.

"Have a seat, Corey."

She shoots me a wary glance as she takes a seat opposite me at my desk. "Did Nico sic you on me?"

I arch a brow. "You're on a first-name basis with my brother?"

"Mr. Tacone," she amends with a slight flush. I love her blushes because they are so at odds with her natural confidence. "No, sorry, not at all. He's dating my cousin, so I just—"

"Ah, yes. *The woman.* The reason Nico called me back from Sicily."

Corey appears taken aback. "What do you mean?"

I wink. "I'm here because he was in danger of losing her—working too many hours. I haven't met her yet, this cousin of yours." I let my gaze travel across Corey's face, down to her enticing cleavage and back. "I can see why he might be enchanted."

No blush this time. In fact, I think she suppressed an eye roll. I really do like this girl. Taming her would be so fun.

"What's her name?"

She crosses her long legs, ease creeping into her

posture. "Sondra. And you probably won't meet her. She's gone."

I knew this already. It's a good thing I arrived when I did because Nico's been completely off the rails since his woman walked out on him. I have yet to see the guy, but I know he's flown home to Chicago to figure out his arranged marriage and other shit with our father.

She tries to take back the lead in the conversation, "So why target me? I'm a good dealer. I keep my nose clean."

My lips twitch. I love her spirit. She's going to be perfect for upstairs. I'll just have to make sure no one touches her because I'm already starting to feel a bit proprietary over the looker. "Your supervisors like you, yes. The ones who aren't jealous." I noticed the female supervisor gave her much lower marks than the males.

The corner of Corey's lips tug up. I like the easy recognition she gives to my statement. She already has correctly interpreted my words and isn't bothered by them. I've already made up my mind—she's smart. Confident. Easy on the eyes. She's perfect.

"We're switching you to higher stakes games. Private ones." I'm not asking; I'm telling. This is the way Tacones do business.

Now I caught her off-guard. Her crimson lips part, and for a moment, no sound comes out. "That sounds dangerous." Her voice strangles slightly on the last word.

I raise a brow, both curious and impressed by her conclusion. "It's not. I'll be there for every game. I won't let anything happen to you." When she remains still, I say, "Or is it me you're worried about?"

Slight blush tells me she's definitely interested, but she

shakes her head. "No. Yes. I guess I mean it sounds... illegal."

There it is. I so appreciate people who can be direct.

I spread my hands. "This is Las Vegas. We have a gambling license. It's the reason my brother moved here."

"Right. Of course." She nods, averting her eyes. I fucking love those little signs of submission on an otherwise alpha female. Like when she apologized for trying to slap me. She knows when to hold her own and when to roll over. It makes me want to flex my dominance in all kinds of filthy ways—put her on her knees and choke her with my cock. Tie her to my bed and keep her screaming all night long. Win her obedience with a whip and a carrot.

She doesn't believe me, which again, shows she's smart. Gambling may not be illegal, but there are all sorts of sordid, underground things that happen around the fringe. Like the sometimes forcible collection of unusual bets placed by desperate men.

This is the game my brother Nico learned from *La Famiglia*. He was a genius to bring it to Vegas, where much of it is legal. Yeah, it means he pays taxes, but believe me, not as much as he should.

"It won't be all the time. Three or four nights a week. We'll double your base pay and the tips should increase, too."

"You're not giving me a choice." It's a statement, not a question.

I wink. "You noticed that, did you? I need you in the upstairs games, Corey. End of story."

Anger flickers in her expression but she quickly hides it. "Why me?"

I lift my shoulders in a casual shrug. "You're professional. Cool and reserved. Trustworthy. Beautiful. In short, you're exactly what I'm looking for."

The wariness in her gaze becomes more apparent. Her dislike of my offer shows on her face, but she says, "Well. I guess I don't have a say in the matter."

I'm slightly surprised. I knew she wasn't a bimbo who'd fall all over herself, flattered, but I don't think I'm giving her a bad deal. And if her cousin's already in bed with Nico—literally—I can't think she has major hangups about our family.

But maybe she does.

"Oh there's always a choice, Ms. Simonson. You can walk out that door."

Eh, I may be the young charming one, but can be as much of a *stronzo* as any of my brothers. Maybe more.

Her dark painted lips compress. "I'm not doing that, Mr. Tacone." Her blue eyes blaze when she meets the challenge in my gaze.

"Good." I stand up and hold out my hand. "Welcome to the big time."

She stands and I note her brief hesitation before taking my hand, but I give her a warm smile as we shake.

"Tomorrow night. Be here by eight."

"Yes, sir. Here—your office?"

I nod, even though it's a terrible idea. I should foist her onto Sal or Leo, tell her somewhere else to meet, but I can't turn down the idea of having her here, in my space. My personal croupier. "Wear a dress—something sexy."

She pauses at the door and turns around, the wariness fully in place again.

"I won't let anyone touch you." I hold up three fingers. "Scout's honor."

Her eyes narrow, lips twist into a smirk. "You were never a Scout." There's a derisive note of knowing in her voice that makes something slide in my belly. The urge to fuck that scorn right off her face combines with the need to punch something.

She's right. I'm no Boy Scout. Never have been. My big brothers were delivering beat-downs on Nico and I before we lost our first baby teeth. We learned the art of violence at the same time we learned our alphabet. Nico perfected the fine art of strategy—how to manipulate and win against the odds—by the time he hit puberty. He showed me the ropes, protected me. My life's been easier than his and I'm not bitter, but I'm also not going to apologize, especially not to this mouthy piece of ass. These are the cards I was dealt, the family I was born into.

But I don't allow any of this to show. Instead, I toss another wink and my lady-killer smile. "You found me out."

I reach past her to open the door again. "Do as you're told—wear the dress. I'll see that you're rewarded." To put a finer point on it, I pull a five-hundred-dollar chip from my pocket and flip it into the air. She catches it, then holds my gaze as she slowly tucks it into her cleavage.

It's all I can do not to slam the door and push her against it, give her a thorough strip-search to see what else she's hiding between or around those perky breasts.

"I'll see you tomorrow, then." Her voice comes out a

little breathy, telling me she's not immune to the heat of my gaze.

I clear my throat. "Tomorrow." I want to slap her ass as she sashays through the door, but I manage to find some self-restraint in time.

Tomorrow, though, she may not be so lucky.

I can't fucking wait to see her in a dress. I already know the sight of her is going to make my night.

Corey

I dial my cousin Sondra on my way out but she doesn't answer. She's with Nico in Chicago after a blowout fight that we all thought had ended things forever. But Tacone has a hard time taking no for an answer. I have to say— Nico Tacone may be a scary motherfucker, but he is totally in deep with Sondra.

When she left him four days ago, he flipped out. He cornered me, tried to make me tell him where she'd gone, put a guy outside my house, presumably to watch for her. Sondra thought he'd been cheating on her. But I talked to everyone close to him after Sondra left, and they all had the same story. He had a family-arranged marriage contract that he was trying to get out of and Sondra is the only woman Nico's ever been serious about.

So when I got her text yesterday with a picture of a diamond ring on her left hand, I knew they'd worked it out.

I really don't know what to think about Sondra

marrying a known mobster. She's always had terrible taste in men—not that my last choice was any better.

But Nico Tacone is the real deal. He's dangerous and powerful. He made my ex disappear. Not that I'm not crying over it. Dean tried to rape my cousin.

But still. Ordinary guys don't have that kind of power.

I'm not judgy about the crime thing. As the daughter of a crooked fed, I have a very jaded sense of crime and law.

But that's why I didn't want to get involved in anything that puts me close to the seedy underbelly of the organization. And the high-stakes private games will definitely do that.

I haven't seen my dad in over ten years. When he left my mom for some skanky chick in Detroit, we all breathed a sigh of relief. Does Stefano know my dad's with the FBI? Somehow I doubt it, and if he finds out, things could get hairy fast.

I really don't know how much illegal activity goes on around here, but I'm guessing it's more peripheral. Why would they need to break laws when their casino rakes in millions a year? Still, I don't want to see any of it. I don't ever want to be in a position where they have to rely on or question my loyalty.

Dammit.

Should I have told Stefano?

And why in the hell am I thinking of him as *Stefano* and not Mr. Tacone? He reprimanded me for calling his brother by his first name.

Oh, maybe it's all the eye-fucking he did. Or the way he kissed my fingers after catching my wrist. A shiver runs through me remembering how quickly he caught and held my wrist without any trace of exertion or anger. Rather, he seemed bemused. As if he enjoyed the opportunity to show me his superior strength and hold me captive.

It's not because I want to be on a first name basis with him.

I definitely don't.

Why would I even think that? Especially after all my concerns for Sondra?

But something about that man has me squeezing my knees together every time he winks. Which is far too often.

I drive home to my small apartment. For the first time since Sondra moved into the casino and Tacone made Dean disappear, it feels too small. Even lonely.

But I'm not looking for company. I don't need to jump into another relationship.

Of course no one's chasing me for one, either. Stefano appears to be the polar opposite of my cousin's possessive and single-minded lover, Nico. He's definitely a player.

Which means sex—just once to get him out of my system—might be on the table.

WANT FREE RENEE ROSE BOOKS?

Click here to sign up for Renee Rose's newsletter and receive a free copy of *Theirs to Protect, Owned by the Marine, Theirs to Punish, The Alpha's Punishment, Disobedience at the Dressmaker's* and *Her Billionaire Boss.* In addition to the free stories, you will also get special pricing, exclusive previews and news of new releases.

THE BOSSMAN SAMPLE - CHAPTER ONE

Please enjoy these sample chapters from **The Bossman***, my earlier mafia series (now available in Kindle Unlimited!)*

Joey La Torre, mafia big-wig and brother to the boss, lay face down on Sophie's massage table, his powerful presence making it impossible to slow her heart rate. He'd shown up without an appointment, stepping into her tiny massage studio as if he owned the place while reminding her he'd been a friend of her father's.

"Would you like to listen to music?" she asked, although it was hard to imagine him enjoying her meditative flute and chant fare.

"Yeah, sure. Whatever you usually do." His voice reverberated around the small room, the rich tones over-filling it the same way his presence had been too large for her waiting room. She averted her eyes from the sight of his sculpted, naked torso, turning on the music and dispensing lavender-scented jojoba oil into her hands.

He flinched when she touched his back, his muscles

only growing tenser as she ran her thumbs up the taut ropes of his erector spinae. Getting him to relax might be an impossibility. He'd explained his physical therapist had recommended massage for the residual pain after a knee replacement. He didn't like strangers touching him, he'd said, but his ma had remembered Artie Palazzo's daughter was a "masseuse."

"Massage therapist," Sophie had corrected.

"Oh yeah? What's the difference?"

"A masseuse isn't licensed, and may be the type that offers happy endings..." she'd trailed off, wishing she hadn't opened that door.

He'd chuckled, but fortunately refrained from making a lewd comment.

She could feel his tension now. She guessed he was the sort of man like her father, who never let his guard down. She leaned her weight into him, using her forearms and even elbows to stroke arcs over his musculature. Joey was all thoroughbred male--wide shoulders, well-defined muscles, olive skin. Though macho men normally turned her off, his physical and charismatic presence combined with the apprehension his unexpected appearance inspired made her panties dampen, even as she cursed his mother for sending him to her.

She'd followed her mother's lead in putting distance between that side of the family and herself since her father's death fifteen years ago. Still, you didn't give offense to Joey La Torre by refusing him service. Besides, she needed the money--her car was on the verge of being repossessed.

She continued her work, surprised when he began to

settle in, responding to her touch and softening. She moved to his lower half, tucking the sheet between his legs to expose one buttock and leg. As she began to rub his glutes, she noticed one of his hips was higher than the other. She moved her fingers to the side of his low back to investigate if the pulling came from the Quadratus lumborum and then froze, realizing the cause of his distortion.

Joey had a hard-on.

Well, shit. Usually when it happened with a client, she ignored it, but with him it felt personal. Though she believed his reason for showing up was legit, she hadn't missed the appreciative once-over he'd given her when he came in and considering how he had laughed when she'd stammered and called him Mr. La Torre, this felt like an opportunity for payback. She smirked and slid her fingers dangerously close to his crack, massaging the inside of his exposed bun, teasing him with her fingers as she worked the insertion of the muscles on the inside of his sit bone. His breath turned ragged and the muscles in his back hardened again. She took her time, slowing torturing him, savoring the feel of his oiled skin, the heady sensation of wielding sexual power. Moving to the other side, she dished out the same intimate treatment, using most of the hour on his buttocks alone.

"It's important to work the hips when the knee hurts," she murmured softly in his ear. "They can get twisted and tightened from the pain."

He gave an unintelligible grunt.

She did have some mercy on him, finishing by placing both hands around the knee, sending energy through her palms until she felt an answering pulse as the energy in the injured joint came alive. "Thank you, Joey," she murmured, touching his shoulder to signal it was over.

He gave a half groan.

She left the treatment room to wait for him, satisfied she'd made him suffer. Just as he emerged, though, she looked out the front window and all gloating vanished. A tow truck lined up next to her car, and the operator got out with a hook.

"Shit!" She opened the door and ran out toward the street. She could not afford to have her car repossessed. "Wait!" she yelled, dashing up to the tow truck. "Please. I'm going to make my payment today."

"Sorry, lady," the guy said without even looking at her.

"Wait--please? Can't you just say you couldn't find it?"

She heard footsteps behind her and cursed, utterly humiliated that Joey La Torre witnessed this degrading scene. The footsteps did not slow, though. Before she understood what was happening, Joey gripped the tow operator by the collar of his coveralls and pointed a pistol at his head.

"No," he snarled. "You heard the lady. You couldn't find it."

The tow guy held up his hands in surrender. "Hey, man, I don't want no trouble, but she hasn't paid her car loan, so this car belongs to the bank. I've got the papers right here," he said, reaching for his pocket. Joey growled in warning, causing the operator to hold his hands up again.

"I'm just gonna get the papers, man."

"Slowly," Joey warned.

The guy reached into his pocket, producing several papers folded together, which he held out with a trembling hand.

She ought to stop him. If she were a better person, she would call him off, or at least attempt to. But the fact was she needed her car, so she kept her mouth shut.

Joey snatched up the papers. "All right, here's what's going to happen. You're going to leave this car here. You're going to tell the bank the loan will be paid off this afternoon. And *you--*" he put his face right up to the other man's, "--you stay away from Joey La Torre's girl. If I ever see you hassling her again, you're a dead man, got it?"

"Yeah, yeah, I got it. I'm sorry, Mr. La Torre. I didn't know she was your girl."

"Don't forget it," Joey growled, releasing the man. "Now get your hook off the car and get the hell out of here."

"Sure thing, Mr. La Torre," he said, scrambling to comply.

Joey stood supervising until the tow truck pulled away, then he turned to her and lifted his chin. "Get inside."

She spread her hands. "Your girl? What the hell?"

He slid his pistol into the holster at his low back.

With the immediate fear of having her car repossessed gone, a new one took hold. She'd be forever beholden to the La Torre mafia now. Why she ever thought she'd be free from the Family was beyond her. "Look, I appreciate your help, but--"

With a hand at her back, he guided her back to her door. She opened her mouth, but before she could speak, he said, "Don't give me grief, Sophie. Go on--do as you're told. Get inside."

She stared at him, her heart pounding a wild rhythm in her chest. She was outraged and humbled and turned on all at the same time. Considering she couldn't do anything with the other two, she opted for humility. "Joey, I can't pay the bank by tomorrow. And I can't pay you back if you meant you were going to pay off the car."

There was no way she was getting into debt with the Mob.

He shrugged. "I'm going to pay off the car." He opened the packet of papers from the tow truck driver and scanned the information.

She rubbed her forehead. She figured she owed over $4,500 with all the late charges and fees tacked on. Tears burned behind her eyes. She didn't want to owe him any favors. If there was one thing she'd learned from her mother, it was once you owed the Family, you belonged to them. "No, I can't allow you to--"

"Shut up. It's not up to you."

Download *The Bossman* and read the rest!

ABOUT RENEE ROSE

USA TODAY BESTSELLING AUTHOR RENEE ROSE loves a dominant, dirty-talking alpha hero! She's sold over a half million copies of steamy romance with varying levels of kink. Her books have been featured in USA Today's *Happily Ever After* and *Popsugar*. Named Eroticon USA's Next Top Erotic Author in 2013, she has also won *Spunky and Sassy's* Favorite Sci-Fi and Anthology author, *The Romance Reviews* Best Historical Romance, and *Spanking Romance Reviews'* Best Sci-fi, Paranormal, Historical, Erotic, Ageplay and favorite couple and author. She's hit the *USA Today* list five times with various anthologies.

Please follow her on:
  Bookbub | Goodreads | Instagram

Renee loves to connect with readers!
www.reneeroseromance.com
reneeroseauthor@gmail.com

OTHER TITLES BY RENEE ROSE

Vegas Underground Mafia Romance

King of Diamonds

Mafia Daddy

Jack of Spades

Ace of Hearts

Joker's Wild

Queen of Hearts (coming soon)

More Mafia Romance

The Russian

The Don's Daughter

Mob Mistress

The Bossman

Contemporary

Black Light: Celebrity Roulette

Blaze: A Firefighter Daddy Romance

Black Light: Roulette Redux

Her Royal Master

The Russian

Black Light: Valentine Roulette

Theirs to Protect

Scoring with Santa

Owned by the Marine

Theirs to Punish

Punishing Portia

The Professor's Girl

Safe in his Arms

Saved

The Elusive "O"

Paranormal

Bad Boy Alphas Series

Alpha's Secret

Alpha's Bane

Alpha's Mission

Alpha's War

Alpha's Desire

Alpha's Obsession

Alpha's Challenge

Alpha's Prize

Alpha's Danger

Alpha's Temptation

Alpha Doms Series

The Alpha's Hunger

The Alpha's Promise

The Alpha's Punishment

Other Paranormals

His Captive Mortal

Deathless Love

Deathless Discipline

The Winter Storm: An Ever After Chronicle

Sci-Fi

Zandian Masters Series

His Human Slave

His Human Prisoner

Training His Human

His Human Rebel

His Human Vessel

His Mate and Master

Zandian Pet

Their Zandian Mate

His Human Possession

Zandian Brides (Reverse Harem)

Night of the Zandians

Bought by the Zandians

Mastered by the Zandians

Zandian Lights

The Hand of Vengeance

Her Alien Masters

Regency

The Darlington Incident

Humbled

The Reddington Scandal

The Westerfield Affair

Pleasing the Colonel

Western

His Little Lapis

The Devil of Whiskey Row

The Outlaw's Bride

Medieval

Mercenary

Medieval Discipline

Lords and Ladies

The Knight's Prisoner

Betrothed

Held for Ransom

The Knight's Seduction

The Conquered Brides (5 book box set)

Renaissance

Renaissance Discipline

Ageplay

Stepbrother's Rules

Her Hollywood Daddy

His Little Lapis

Black Light: Valentine's Roulette (Broken)

BDSM under the name Darling Adams

Medical Play

Yes, Doctor

Master/Slave

Punishing Portia

Made in the USA
Monee, IL
17 June 2021

71365768R00143